A Killing in a Small Town

A novel

By Scott Fields

Outer Banks Publishing Group

Outer Banks/Raleigh

www.outerbankspublishing.com

For ordering information contact Outer Banks Publishing Group at
info@outerbankspublishing.com

FIRST EDITION
ISBN 10 - 0990679004
ISBN 13 - 978-0-9906790-0-4
eISBN: 978-1311327079

October 2014

Also by Scott Fields

It was the worse two-week killing spree in Ohio's history. On the night of July 21, 1948, Robert Daniels and John West entered John and Nolena Niebel's house and forced the family into their car and drove them to a cornfield just off Fleming Falls Road in Mansfield. Robert Daniels then shot each of them in the head. The brutal murders caught national attention in the media, but the killing spree didn't stop there. Three more innocent people would lose their lives at the hands of Daniels and West in the coming week.

Scott Fields tirelessly researched the killings, the capture and trial of Daniels and even interviewed a surviving member of the Niebel family to weave this tragic story into a must-read novel bringing the reader back to those dark days in the summer of 1948. It has been more than sixty years since the tragedy, and, yet, the why of it all still remains unanswered.

The killing spree is not only remembered to this day, but is an important and dark part of Mansfield lore.

Summer Heat

If you read Fifty Shades of Grey, you'll like Summer Heat! When she was 17, there wasn't a man alive she would let get near her, and when she was 18, there wasn't a man she would keep away.

Women universally hated her, men continued to hold doors for her long after she passed by - just to watch her walk away.

Ninety-nine point nine percent of the men in Steam Corners wanted her, but she only wanted one man, Spencer Deacon. The one thing that Spencer didn't want was Jessie, and his firm and undeniable rejections infuriated her.

What followed was a series of sordid events involving murder, deceit, betrayal and the conviction of an innocent man.

Both books are available on Amazon in print and as an ebooks as well as available from Barnes & Noble and fine bookstores everywhere.

CHAPTER 1

A late model corvette with faded paint jumped the curb in front of a white Victorian house. Carrying a half-empty bottle of Jack Daniels, Harlan Steelman fell out of his car and stumbled across the perfectly manicured lawn. He sucked down the remaining contents of the bottle and tossed it onto the lawn. He wiped his mouth with the back of his hand, staggering backwards on the lawn.

A dark sedan backed slowly out of the garage and stopped at the end of the driveway. His hand still resting on the gearshift, the driver glared at the man standing in his front yard. Smiling defiantly, Harlan turned to face the man in the car. The driver dropped the gearshift into Drive and shifted his foot from the brake to the accelerator. He clenched the steering wheel as the car inched forward.

"You ain't got the nerve!" shouted Harlan weaving from side-to-side.

The driver's foot flinched. The car leaped forward and stopped with the two front tires resting on the grass.

Harlan laughed aloud. He bent over and peered into the car. "Come and get me," he shouted as he taunted the driver. "For once in your life have a spine!"

The man leaned forward in his seat. His eyebrows were furrowed; his lips set in a straight line. "You son-of-a-bitch!" he shouted aloud. The car rolled forward and stopped. Moments passed. The two men stared at each other with only snickers from Harlan.

Suddenly, Harlan stood upright, unzipped his pants, and began to urinate on the lawn. "Hey, Dumbass!" he shouted. "I hear this ain't good for your lawn!" He finished and laughed hysterically as he hopped on one leg across the lawn trying unsuccessfully to zip his pants.

The driver of the car slammed the gearshift into Reverse and floored the accelerator. The car careened into the street, stopped, and sped away.

Harlan watched as the car disappeared around the corner. "Need to slow down," he muttered staring at the empty street. "Someone's going to get hurt." He turned and started for the front door tripping over the first step. "Shit!" he shouted.

The front door creaked open. "Get the hell in here!" shouted a hushed voice. Harlan did not move. "Hurry up and get in here!"

The young man got to his feet and grabbed the door handle to steady himself. He opened the door and fell inside. A young woman dressed in a nightgown and robe slammed the door behind him. "Damn, I wish you wouldn't do that," she said peeking through the curtains.

"Do what?" Harlan slurred.

The young woman turned and started for the kitchen. She was a slender woman with soft and ample femininity. "You can at least wait 'till he's gone to work," she said covering herself with her robe.

Harlan closed his eyes and leaned against the wall. He was a tall man with slim features. He had a rugged-looking face that, except for a scar that ran from his left ear to his jaw, was handsome enough to win him rights to bedrooms all over town. "What makes the difference," he said staggering across the room. "He ain't gonna do anything to me anyhow," he said as he fell onto the sofa.

"He's going to shoot you one of these days," she said carrying two cups of coffee into the room.

"I don't think he knows which end of a gun to hold," said Harlan slouching on the couch. "Besides, he ain't got the nerve, and you know it."

The woman set one of the cups on a table and began sipping from the other. "Every man has his breaking point, Harlan, and you know it," she said sitting down beside him. "Lord knows there's enough men in this town who should be there because of you."

Harlan picked up his coffee, stared at it for a moment, and set it back down. "Damn, I'm tired," he said leaning his head back.

"By the way," she said turning in his direction, "what's got you so worked up? Can't remember when I've seen you drunk this early in the morning."

Harlan didn't answer. A raucous noise came from his open mouth, and he woke up. "What?" he slurred.

"What's got you drinking so early in the morning?"

"Morning? Hell, this is the end of last night," he said leaning forward and running his hands through his hair. "I ain't been home yet."

"Jesus, Harlan, aren't you getting a little old for this?" she said sipping her coffee. Harlan said nothing. "By the way, can't you at least park down the street? The neighbors have enough to talk about without you giving them more fuel for the fire."

"They're just jealous," he said with a smile. "They just wish my car was parked in front of their house." He slid across the couch and put his arm around the woman. "Besides, I didn't come over here to talk about your old man or the neighbor ladies. Give me some sugar."

"No, Harlan," she said getting to her feet. "Not today. You're drunk and you stink like a hog."

Harlan got to his feet. "Oh, come on, baby," he said grabbing each of her arms. "You can't tell me you don't want it. You always want it."

"Oh, yes, I can tell you that," she said breaking his grip and stepping away. "I want you to go now."

Harlan grabbed her tightly with both hands. "I don't think you understand," he said with determination. "I didn't come here for any of your crap. Now, give it to me."

"You're hurting me," she said struggling to get free.

Harlan wrapped his arms around her and began kissing the side of her neck. "Just want some lovin'," he mumbled.

The woman lifted her knee and caught him in the crotch.

"Goddamn!" he shouted as he stepped back. He bent at the waist and held his hands between his legs. He glared at the woman standing in front of him. "You'll pay for that, you bitch!" he shouted and started across the room.

The long winter had ended, and the warm summer winds blew. The young man of nearly sixteen years of age cocked the handle of his Daisy BB gun and searched the tall trees for a would-be target. His eyes slowly scanned the foliage searching for any telltale movement of some unwitting prey. An unusually large blue jay came to rest on a branch of a maple tree nearly fifty feet away. The bird nervously jerked his head from side to side searching for some form of sustenance on the ground below. The young man studied the bird for a moment and then slowly lifted the weapon and carefully nestled the stock of the gun in his shoulder. He pointed the barrel of the rifle at his prey and moved it slightly until the sights were centered on its bright blue breast. He slowly squeezed the trigger. There was a dull report and slight recoil as the weapon fired its projectile. Just below the branch that the bird was resting on, there was a scattering of leaves as the BB fell short of its mark sending the frightened bird into a hasty escape.

"Shit!" shouted the boy. He cocked the gun again as he watched the bird fly out of sight. "Damn gun never did work right," he muttered aloud. He shouldered the rifle and began to search the trees for another target.

Summer had finally come to the small town of Little Falls, Michigan. It had been a long and hard winter as most winters are in that part of the country. The warmth of summer was only a slight respite from the harsh and brutal winds of the long and cold winters.

Little Falls was a small mining town carved out of the thick pines of the Upper Peninsula of Michigan. Two trappers founded the town at the end of the nineteenth century as a result of the discovery of gold. As the news spread through the lower part of the state, there was a frenzied exodus as would be fortune-seekers made their way to the northern wilderness. Shopkeepers, trappers, businessmen alike abandoned their trades and began the arduous journey to claim their share of the bounty.

However, fortune and wealth were not to be found in this primitive part of the country. The quickly built mine yielded only a trace of the valuable ore and was soon closed after a collapse killed three men.

By then, hundreds of people had risked everything to make the trip, and there was no turning back. Construction of a new mine soon began while others panned the cold, clear streams that wandered, aimlessly, through this wooded country. Housing construction began, as did the erection of buildings for the purpose of trade, and soon a town was born. The dream of fame and fortune soon vanished, and the discovery of gold was soon forgotten in the small town of Little Falls. Fortunes would have to be made by other means.

The seemingly inexhaustible supply of pine trees became the source of revenue for the small young town. Fortunes were made by a few, and steady employment was enjoyed by many. Little Falls had been born and over the years would swell to over a thousand people. The lumber industry continued to be the only source of income for its inhabitants for nearly seventy years. Prosperity rose and fell with market prices, but the town continued to survive.

There wasn't much for a teenager to do in Little Falls. The nearest bowling alley and Movie Theater was thirty miles away in Bear Creek, and unless you had a driver's license and the loan of the family sedan, you were destined to create your own entertainment. The only television station whose broadcast could be received in Little Falls was located in Ludington over seventy miles away. Most nights, the reception was good and the picture was clear. Yet, it seemed like every night when something good was on the picture was fuzzy and faded in and out. Reruns of The Lawrence Welk Show came in perfectly clear.

The young man sighted down the barrel of the rifle as he scanned the trees above. There were no birds. It was as if they had all disappeared for some reason. There was an eerie silence as if all living things had left the area.

Suddenly, there was a metallic clatter. The young man spun around to find a young black bear about fifty feet away bent over a metal trash can in search of food. He froze in his tracks as he stared at the animal. Apparently, he remained undetected for the animal continued to forage for food in spite of his obvious presence.

Slowly, he inched his way to a small sapling that offered partial concealment. He watched intently as the animal strew papers and cans over the ground. It would occasionally pause for a moment as it devoured some treasure it had found at the bottom of an open can or package.

Black bears were common for this part of the country. Over the past ten years their population had nearly doubled, and as their numbers increased, so did the frequency of contact with humans. In spite of their foreboding and ferocious nature, most black bears prefer to avoid any confrontation with people. Unless they feel threatened or feel a need to protect their young, most bears simply turn and run away.

However, not all contact with these wild animals was without incidents. There were stories of bear attacks that had been passed down from one generation to another that were grossly embellished with each telling. As the years passed, the stories evolved into legends of incomparable feats and events. They were now dismissed as myth and fantasy by many of the townspeople but still regarded and lauded as a cultural inheritance by all.

Most children were taught at an early age to avoid confrontation of any kind. In spite of their usual docile appearance, bears of all kind are easily provoked, and in spite of their incredible bulk, they can easily outrun any human. Most children regarded their parents' admonitions very seriously and indeed acquired a deep and abiding respect for the animal. However, there were exceptions over the years, and from them were born the legends of yore.

"You're sure enough making a mess out of that trash can," muttered the young man. "Pop's going to kill me. I was supposed to bury that garbage."

By now, the animal had tipped the can over onto the ground and was using its claw to rake the contents from the container.

"You have got to go," he warned in a somewhat louder voice. He pointed the gun at the animal and squinted down the length of the barrel. The two notches were aligned and centered on the bear's shoulder. He gently squeezed the trigger. The gun fired, and the BB found its mark. The animal grunted and leaned back on his hind legs. The BB had not broken the skin but had produced a sting not unlike that which is felt from a wasp or a bee.

The bear turned in the boy's direction. It grunted again as it stared at the now fully exposed boy. Its fur ruffled giving it a much bigger appearance. Its face took on an angry look with eyes that were hidden in two deep caves of fur. It then gave forth a deep and menacing growl that warned of impending attack, fell forward on all four legs, and began to run in the boy's direction.

The young man dropped his gun and started for the backdoor of their house. It was a fifty yard sprint, and he was pumping his legs as fast as he could. Huge legs pounded the earth behind him, breathing that growled with each gulp of air. The animal was gaining on him. He could tell it. He was nearing the halfway point, and already his lungs were on fire.

Suddenly, a voice boomed across the backyard. "Run, Travis! Run like you never ran before!"

The young man looked up to see his father standing on the back porch aiming a double-barrel shotgun in his direction. He put his head down and gathered strength to run even faster.

The man on the porch tilted the barrel of the gun into the air and pulled one of the triggers. An explosion ripped through the evening sky sending birds and animals fleeing in every direction. The charging bear stiffened his front legs, digging his front claws into the soft earth. He nearly tumbled forward as he skidded to a stop. Travis finished his flight with a ten-foot leap to the safety of the porch.

"Get behind me!" he shouted to his son.

The bear had completely stopped. It gasped for air as it stood motionless just twenty feet from the house glaring into the man's eyes.

John lowered the gun until the barrel was pointing at the beast in front of him. He pulled back the hammer on the loaded barrel and clicked it in place. The bear did not move.

John took aim. Then, as if the animal understood the seriousness of the situation, it slowly but deliberately turned around and lumbered away.

When the animal finally disappeared from sight, John turned to his son. He leaned the shotgun against the house and placed a hand on the young man's shoulder. He bent over to look him in the eyes. "Son, do you know what you did wrong here?" he asked.

"Yeah, don't ever shoot a bear with a BB gun," he replied.

John paused as he stared at his son in disbelief. "You shot at a bear with a BB gun?"

"You mean you didn't know?"

John paused as he stared at his son. He slowly dropped his arms to his sides. "Why in the world would you shoot a 400 pound bear with a BB gun?" he asked.

Travis glanced in the direction of the trashcan. "I thought I might scare him away," he replied.

John leaned back and placed his hands on his hips. He was a big man nearly six and a half feet tall. A lifetime of hard work had left him with a lean, muscular body that was admired by many and feared by most. "You thought you might scare him away, did you?" asked John. "Tell me something, son. Did you learn anything today?"

"You're darn right I did, Pop," said Travis still gasping for air.

"And what is that?"

"Keep my mouth shut so I don't get in any more trouble."

"Do you know what you really did wrong, son?"

"I didn't bury the garbage like you told me."

"Guess what," said John with a smile. "With that correct answer, you won a free dinner. Now, go wash up."

The young man opened the screen door and let it slam behind him. "What's for dinner?" he shouted as he raced across the kitchen floor. He began to wash his hands as his mother carried bowls of food to the table.

"We're having chicken and mashed potatoes with gravy," she announced with pride.

"Chicken!" he shouted. "That sounds great, but don't we usually have chicken on Sundays? What's the occasion?"

"No special reason," she replied as she set a pitcher of water on the table. "Just seemed like we needed a change. You know what I mean, Travis? Sometimes, it seems like a body can get into a rut, and you need to do things different."

Travis looked into his mother's face. The smile was gone. Something was bothering her. He could tell. She had a forever smile that announced to the world that everything was all right, but today was different.

Kara was an attractive woman. She was just into her thirties but still maintained a youthful appearance. She had a robust and shapely figure that still turned heads and a certain twinkle in her deep blue eyes that had seduced more than one man in her life.

Today, she wore a faded and frayed dress that had been new longer ago than she could remember. It had buttons down the front that strained from the age of the garment opening gaps that revealed her soft skin.

"I smell chicken!" shouted John as he headed for the sink to wash his hands. "What's going on? Did I miss something? Is it Sunday already?"

"Mom's in a rut," Travis announced as he poured himself a glass of water. "She needs a change."

"So, momma needs a change, does she?" he asked as he dried his hands on a towel. "Well, I got news for you. We're in for a big change and real soon."

"What are you talking about?" she asked as she turned in his direction. "What kind of change?"

John's eyes fell to her bosom. He studied the front of her dress. "You don't have a bra on!" he exclaimed in a whisper. "What's the matter with you? I can see your...your bosoms."

"My only bra broke this morning when I put it on," she whispered. "Besides, it feels kind of good to do without."

"Have you gone crazy?" he asked in a louder voice. "You can't go running around here like that. It ain't normal."

"Ain't nobody going to see me," she replied. "No one ever comes to this house. Don't ever answer the door when they do for fear it might be a bill collector. Besides, it could be worse. I hear that Marge Cooper does her housework in the nude. Not a stitch on. Somebody said that it don't matter if someone comes to the door. She still doesn't cover up."

"Good God, woman!" he shouted. "Marge Cooper is as crazy as a loon! They say she's seeing some head doctor over in Bear Creek every Thursday. Something must be wrong with her if she'd marry that travelling salesman like she did. I don't think she's but nineteen, and that guy is old enough to be her father." John dried his hands on a dishcloth and returned it to the handle on the stove.

"By the way, what was all the shooting about?" asked Kara taking her seat at the table.

John turned to the young man sitting at the table. Travis had a look of shock as he turned to his father. "Oh, nothing special," he replied with a wink to his son. "Just scaring away the crows." John took his seat, and they all began to eat.

Minutes later, John finished his meal and gently pushed his empty plate aside. He carefully folded his hands and placed them on the table. "I have an announcement to make," he said with a smile. "I've lost my job again."

"You did what?" asked Kara.

"I know what you're thinking," said John. "But it wasn't my fault this time."

"It's never your fault," said Kara getting up from the table. She walked across the kitchen and stood in front of the sink looking out the window. "It's always somebody or something else, isn't it, John? What happened this time? Did your boss say something, or did you just get tired of working there?"

John got up from his chair and walked across the floor. "Don't be like this, Kara," he said easing a hand on her shoulder. "We're going to be alright. You'll see."

"That's what you always say, John," she said bowing her head and leaning on the sink. "But it never does. It never gets any better."

"Don't be like this, Kara," he said. "We're doing alright, aren't we?"

"Doing alright!" she said loudly. She turned to John. "You can't be serious! We don't own a thing. We rent this house and everything in it. We don't even own our own sofa. So, don't tell me we're doing alright."

The room became silent. John pulled back and leaned against the sink. He glanced over at Travis who was holding his head in his hands. He turned back to the woman beside him. "I just wanted you to know that I have a plan," he announced.

"What is it this time?" she asked. "What kind of plan do you have in mind this time?"

"Tomorrow, we pack up the old Ford, and we're going back to Bear Creek."

Kara stood straight and turned to her husband. She stared at him with a puzzled look. "Bear Creek," she said. "You said we'd never go back there."

"I know that's what I said, but I think we need a new start, and I figure what better place to do it than in your own hometown."

Kara turned and leaned against the sink. She stared blankly at the wall. A smile soon appeared on her face. "Okay," she said still staring at the wall. "Let's do it."

CHAPTER 2

The morning sun was already high in the sky when the last piece of luggage was strapped to the top of the car. John walked around the old Ford one last time to check each knot for tightness.

"All right, everybody," he said as he opened the driver's side door. "Let's go." Kara stood for several moments and stared at the house. She was lost in a river of forgotten memories and dreams. She climbed into the car and turned to watch as they pulled slowly away from the curb. She would never see that house again, and she knew it.

It was only thirty miles to Bear Creek and was normally a quick trip. The only road to Bear Creek seldom had any traffic, but today it took John nearly an hour. He drove very slowly to avoid losing any of their belongings. As they entered the city limits, John slowed the vehicle even more. People stared as they drove down the neighborhood street. A small dog began to chase the car barking loudly as if to alert the others of the approaching sight.

"Things have changed," Kara muttered as she glanced at the houses on both sides of the street.

"Oh, I don't know," said John. "There's old man Henshaw sitting on his front porch just like he did fifteen years ago. He's just a little fatter. That's all."

The old car came to a stop at a traffic light near the downtown area. Many of the people who were crossing at the intersection stopped and stared at the heavily laden car.

Bear Creek was a small town with just over a thousand residents. The business area consisted of two hardware stores, two grocery stores, one gas station, and several other small businesses. Nothing much had changed in the past fifteen years. Because of the economy, very few improvements had been made to the businesses or the homes. It was as if time had stood still.

"Why is everyone staring at us, John?" asked Kara.

"I don't know," he replied. "Maybe, they're trying to figure out who we are. Don't forget. People in this town never did take to strangers."

"I don't like it, John," she said as she covered her face with her hand. "Get me out of here."

John looked up to see the light turn green and eased out the clutch. "Everything will be alright," he said as he turned the corner that led to downtown.

"John, you never did tell me where we're going," she said turning in his direction. "You said you called Harry Miller. What could he possibly do for us?"

"Harry retired a few years back and closed his service station. He said it would be alright for us to park in back," said John.

"In back of what?"

"In back of his service station."

"Why? Why would we want to park back there?"

"For privacy. At least back there, most people won't see us much."

Kara grew silent. She turned and stared at her husband. A look of anger swept over her face. "Don't tell me, John," she said in a stern voice. "You don't expect us to live in a car, do you?"

"It's only for awhile. It's just until I can find a job and a place to live. It'll be all right. I promise."

"You can't be serious, John," she shouted. "People don't live in cars. We'll be the laughing stock of town."

"It will only be for a short time."

"What's a short time, John? Are you talking about days, weeks, or months? Where are we supposed to clean up? We can't live in a car without staying clean. It just isn't sanitary."

"Harry said he would leave the restrooms unlocked," said John turning down a side street. "We can use them all we want as long as we keep them clean."

"Keep them clean!" shouted Kara turning in his direction. "Can you imagine what they must look like?" She folded her arms and turned away. "John, I refuse to use them filthy toilets."

"Kara, don't be that way," said John bringing the car to a stop. "We'll clean the restrooms. You'll see. Everything's going to be just fine." He turned and looked out the window.

"Besides, we're home." The two other occupants turned to see their new home.

It was the back of Harry Miller's gas station. When it was open for business, few people stopped because of the condition of the building and surrounding area. It was a concrete block building that had never been painted. Vines climbed wildly on all sides of the building, as they seem to take possession of the now deserted building. Rusted car parts were scattered over the lot partially hidden by the weeds that were now out of control.

"See, I told you we'd have privacy," said John pointing out the window. "We got a big fence on this side and a church on the other. Ain't nobody going to see anything except maybe on Sundays, and those people aren't interested in seeing us."

For a moment, the young woman stared out the window. She then bowed her head and began to cry. "John, you promised better than this," she sobbed. "You promised that we would live like other folks. You can't do this, John. It just ain't right."

Silence followed. John stared at his wife and then turned to the young man in the back seat. "Travis, why don't you go take a look around?"

"What's there to see?" he asked.

John turned and pointed out the back window. "You see that road over there?" he asked. "Just follow that until it takes you out of town. About a mile from here, you'll cross a river. Best darn swimming hole in the county."

"Sounds great, Pop," he said as he opened the car door. "I'll be back after a while." He closed the door behind him and started down the road. He knew there would soon be a fight between his parents, and he would rather be someplace else.

It was a hot and lazy summer day. The cool sidewalk felt good to the young man's bare feet. He slowly walked past the grocery store, the small pharmacy, and the library. Three older men sat on a bench in front of the Sinclair gas station. They whispered and pointed as they studied the young man walking by.

The sidewalk stopped at the edge of town, and Travis soon found himself on a country road that led out of town. The tall pine trees stood like sentries at attention. The young man passed an open field that had been carved out of the thick growth of trees. Green corn stalks stood nearly knee-high. Their elongated leaves seemed to softly bounce on the soft summer breeze and wave at the young man as he walked by.

Travis stopped at the edge of the South Bridge. It was a slightly rusted steel structure that spanned the swiftly moving Clear Fork River. He walked down to the river's edge and watched as the muddy green water flowed by. It had been a rainy spring, and most of the rivers in the area were at their crest.

He began to walk downstream picking his way through bushes and undergrowth until he came to spot where the river had widened. The rapid flow of the water seemed to lessen as it spilled into this small pool. It was clear that the water was deep at this point. Currents of water flowed in all directions while swirling eddies created whirlpools that reached to the bottom of the river.

Travis leaned over and thrust his hand into the murky water. It was icy cold to the touch. He stood upright rubbing his two hands together. He looked one way and then the other. It was quiet. The only sound was the distant rushing of water. The young man paused as he listened. It sounded like a waterfall somewhere in the distance.

Travis stripped down to his underwear and carefully laid his clothes on a rock. He tipped-toed down to the edge of the water and slowly eased one foot into the murky slime. "Damn!" he shouted as he recoiled his foot from the cold water. The young man stared at the water for a moment. He glanced both ways and bent down in a crouched position. "Here goes," he muttered and jumped legs first into the river.

"Jesus, God!" he screamed as he body plunged into the cold water. He splashed the water violently with his hands as he jumped up and down. In a few moments, his body adjusted to the cold, and he became quiet, his feet resting on the muddy bottom.

Travis spun around as he surveyed the river. He couldn't believe that his father described this as a great place to swim. It was dirty, and the current was so fast that he could hardly stand in one spot. It was so deep that in some places it nearly reached his armpits. It was primitive, but for some unknown reason, Travis considered it to be a place of beauty. Tall, maKaratic oak and elm trees crowded proudly together along the banks of the river. As if in a display of respect, they bowed their heads forming a vaulted arch ceiling that seemed to cover the river as far as could be seen. A small dead branch fell from its lofty home into the river below. Travis turned in the direction of the noise that echoed down the corridor formed by the banks of the river. The small branch seemed to come alive as it twisted and turned in the wild but steady current. "Oh, my God, it's a snake!" he exclaimed as he studied the fast approaching object. He stared intently until he noticed several leaves that were stubbornly hanging onto a small twig growing from the back of the branch. The young man sighed and relaxed as he watched the floating piece of wood drift near the opposite bank and snag itself on a fallen tree that lay partly in the water.

By now, Travis had adjusted to the cold water and decided to take a swim. He leaned forward and began to paddle to the other shore. The current was strong, but the young man was able to maintain his course. He soon reached the muddy bottom of the bank, turned, and pushed off. This time he decided to make it more challenging by swimming underwater. He took a deep breath and submerged under the cold murky water. He struggled against the strong current, paddling as hard as he could. After a few moments, he returned to the surface, gulping fresh air as he gained his footing on the river bottom.

From behind Travis came a voice that said, "Hey, kid." He spun around in the water, and there standing at the river's edge was a young boy about his own age. He was a handsome young man with dress pants and shirt. He was lean in stature, almost frail, and yet he had a wily look about him that was almost menacing.

"Who are you?" asked the intruder pulling a pocketknife from his pocket.

"I'm Travis Watson," the young man replied. "Who are you?"

"You're a part of that bunch that is living in a car, aren't you?" he asked unfolding the blade of the knife.

"How the hell do you know that already?" asked Travis. "We just got into town."

"The old man who owns that gas station is Harry Miller. I heard him telling my dad about you people."

"You still haven't answered my question. Who the hell are you?"

"My name is Melvin Steelman. Now, you answer mine. You live in a car, don't you?"

Travis scanned the riverbank as if searching for an answer. "It's just temporary," he muttered.

"Your old man is out of work, and you don't have a pot to piss in," blurted Melvin as he began to clean under his fingernails with the small knife.

Travis grew silent. He glared at the young man standing by the river's edge. "Is there a point to all this, or are you just a natural-born asshole?" he asked.

"Who are you calling an asshole?"

"You. Who else?"

"You live in a car, and you call me an asshole."

"Let me guess. You're some rich faggot living in some big mansion. Am I right?"

Melvin leaned back. "My daddy has lots of money, if that's what you mean," he said returning the knife to his pocket.

"That's no surprise."

"Why do you say that?"

"Because you're a snob. That's why. All rich people are snobs, and you're a snob."

"What would you know about snobs or rich people for that matter?" asked Melvin picking up a stone and throwing it in the river.

"My Pop told me," said Travis as he slapped the surface of the water sending a spray of water in Melvin's direction.

"Your Pop? Is that what you call your father? Pop? Somehow that figures. People who live in cars, I'm sure, talk like that. Besides, what would your old man know about rich people? I'll bet your mother could make more money on her back than your old man ever did."

"Why you son of a ..." said Travis as he started wading to shore. "You wait right there until I get out of the water."

Melvin leaned over and grabbed Travis' shirt and pants. He leaned back and hurled them into the river. Travis watched as the clothing sailed through the air and landed in the center of the river. The swift current immediately grabbed the clothes and dragged them away.

Travis turned to the young man standing at the river's edge. "You'll pay for this, you son-of-a-bitch," he said shaking his fist.

"You have to catch me first, asshole," said Melvin as he turned and began to run away.

"You're going to get the whipping of your life. I promise you. I'm sure your sissy ass never had an ass kicking from a junkyard dog like me.

Travis retrieved his clothes and got out of the water. He put on his soaking wet shirt and pants and started for home.

It was late afternoon when the young man returned to the family automobile. "What's there to eat?" he asked opening the rear car door.

"I fixed you a sandwich," his mother replied. "Get in and close the door."

"Great! I'm starved!" he announced as he grabbed the food.

"My God, son. What happened to you? Did you fall into the river?"

"I had a little problem. That's all," he said taking a bite from his sandwich. "Nothing to be concerned about." Travis looked into his mother's eyes. Something was wrong. She had been crying. Her eyes were red and she had been blowing her nose. "Where's Dad?"

"He went for a walk," she said without looking up. "We had a big fight, and he needed to get away for awhile."

"I wish you and Pop wouldn't fight," said Travis taking a drink of water. "Everything is going to be just fine, Ma. I just know it."

"I wish I could believe you, son. I really do," she said turning around in her seat. "It just seems that we are always taking one step forward and three back."

"We'll be ok, Ma. You'll see."

One of John's shirts was draped over the car seat. Kara took one of the sleeves and wiped her eyes. "I'm not asking for much," she said softly as if she were thinking aloud. "I just want a place to call my own. Some place where I can unpack all the boxes. Do you know what I mean, Travis? I want to buy furniture. My God, it ain't right to be my age and never owned any furniture."

"We'll get some furniture, Ma. You'll see. Things are going to be different here. I can feel it."

"You know what my real dream is, don't you, Travis?" she asked with a smile. "My real dream is to have a room all to myself. Can you imagine? A room for my very own and I don't mean a bedroom. I mean a room where I can go when I need to get away. A sitting room, I think they call it. The best part is that it would be all mine. Neither you nor your father would be allowed in there. Of course if you knocked and asked politely, I would allow you to visit me in my room, but you could never go there by yourself." Kara stared out the window of the car. Travis took another bite from his sandwich. It became quiet in the car.

"Oh, my," she muttered turning away from the window. "How I go on. How do you put up with me?"

"Everything is going to be okay, Ma. You'll see. You're just a little upset with Pop. That's all."

"I don't know what's wrong with me," she said as she straightened the bags of food and clothes in the front seat. "It's not just your dad and me. I'm not sure what it is." She turned and gave Travis a quick glance. "Besides, I shouldn't be talking to you about this."

"Why not, Mother?"

"It ain't right. That's all. It just ain't right."

"Do you still love Pop?"

"What?"

"Do you still love Pop?"

"Sure I do," she replied turning away. "I've always loved your dad. We might have had our differences, but we never stopped loving each other. I just seem to be a little restless lately. I suppose I'll get over it. I always do." She glanced out the window. "Now, off with you. Your father is coming back, and I need to talk to him."

Travis climbed out of the car and started running down the street. "Bye!" he screamed as he turned down a side street.

"Was that our son?" asked John as he opened the door and slid across the seat.

"Yes. He has something to do," she replied. "Where have you been?"

"I went for a walk," he said turning in his seat to face Kara. "I think I have good news. I think I have a job."

"Where?" she asked looking up.

"Do you remember Howard Bailey who owns the hardware store? He told me to stop down tomorrow morning. He said he might be able to use me."

"That's wonderful, John."

"I'm telling you, Kara, things are going to get better for us. Just you wait and see."

"I hope so," she said. "I really do." She glanced down at her lap and fumbled with the material on her dress. "You know, John, I've been thinking. Ever since daddy died, mother hasn't been doing so well. I was thinking that maybe I should take Travis and go and live with her for a while. You know. Just long enough until mother is feeling better." She paused and looked up at her husband. "What do you think?"

John turned with a frown. "You want to move away from here?" he asked.

"Just for a short time."

"No way in the world!" he shouted. "We are a family, and families stick together."

"It will just be for a couple weeks."

"No!" shouted John. "You're staying here with me! I won't hear of it!"

Kara glanced down at her tired hands. She sighed and turned to the window. A lone tear streaked down her cheek. "I know I should be a better wife," she said wiping her face. I know I should be more supportive and understanding. It's just that everything seems to go bad for us any more. We don't ever seem to get a break."

John took a deep breath and ran his fingers through his hair. "Come on, Kara," he said placing a hand on her knee. "Things aren't that bad. We'll be alright."

"Things aren't that bad?" questioned Kara pushing his hand away. "John, look at us. You don't have a job, and we live in a car. That's not normal, John. Look around you. Do you see anyone else living in a car? People don't live like this." She turned her head and began to cry.

"Things will get better, Kara," said John. "I promise."

"I don't even own a chair to sit in," she muttered without turning around.

Silence followed. John turned to stare out the window. Kara dried her eyes and turned to John. "What are we going to do about you and me?" she asked.

"What are you talking about?"

"You know what I'm talking about."

"Do you mean sex?"

"You know I can't go long without it."

"For God's sakes, Kara," he said turning in her direction. "We don't have enough problems that you have to invent one more?"

"Well, what are we going to do, John? We can't do anything with Travis there in the back seat."

John gave his wife a quick glance. "I don't know, Karas," he said turning away. "We'll figure something out."

The young woman slid across the seat. "What's wrong with right now?" she asked placing her hand on his.

John paused as he stared at his wife. He turned the door handle and opened the car door. "Christ, woman," he said stepping out of the car. "You need professional help. I have something to do. I'll be back later," he said and walked away.

CHAPTER 3

The next morning brought a bright orange sun climbing proudly into a blue sky. The air was crisp following the torrents of rain from the night before. Sunlight poured through the streaked window sending ghost-like shadows on the floor. A cool breeze sent the soft curtains swaying hypnotically in and out.

A young man reached down to the side of the bed and raked a match across the sideboard. It roared to life as he held it under the tip of a cigarette.

"Jesus, Harlan, I wish you wouldn't do that," said the woman lying next to him. She pulled the bed sheet over her breasts as she leaned over for a cigarette.

Harlan threw the spent match at a wastebasket across the room. He leaned forward as he began to cough violently. Mucous gurgled, and he expelled it onto the floor.

"My God!" shouted the woman sitting up in bed. "Did you just spit on my floor?"

Harlan glanced around the room. It was ornately furnished in Victorian décor. "You didn't expect me to swallow that mess, did you?" he asked turning in her direction.

The woman settled back into bed. "You know if you're going to spit on my floor and do what you did to me last night, I'm not going to invite you over here anymore," she said with a smile.

Harlan inhaled his cigarette and smiled. "Mavis, I counted twelve orgasms last night," he said expelling the smoke over his head. "God knows how many you really got."

Mavis smiled. "I lost count somewhere along the way."

"Honey, there ain't no way you're going to give that up," he said as he turned and sat on the edge of the bed. Harlan was a young man just 28 years of age with a rugged face and a lean body. His upper lip had a slight upturn giving him a sneer that started more than a few bar fights.

"I got to get going," he said running his fingers through his hair. "I have business in town to take care of."

"Oh yeah," said Mavis drawing on her cigarette. "Just use me and run off. Just like a man."

Harlan pulled a dirty white sock over his size twelve foot. "Who used who?" he asked. "Christ, I didn't get no forty orgasms last night."

"I feel so cheap," she said rolling over on one side. "You could at least talk to me for a while."

Harlan pulled on his denim jeans and stood to zip them. "Have you heard about the new super sensitive condom?" he asked buttoning his shirt. Mavis said nothing. "It hangs around after the man leaves and talks to the woman," he said sticking his shirttail in his pants.

He turned to the woman still lying in bed. She smiled and then snorted in an effort to hold back laughter.

"You're an asshole!" she shouted and threw a slipper in his direction.

"Yes, but you love me," he said with a smile.

Mavis sighed. "Yes, you're right there," she muttered. "I truly do that. When will I see you again? Probably not 'till you get horny again."

"How long is the old man going to be out of town?"

"He'll be back on Friday."

Harlan paused. "I should be back before he gets home. Where is the Counselor this week? Is he in some legal battle defending all the good people of the earth?"

"I don't know, and I don't care," she snapped.

"Nice talk," said Harlan starting for the door. "God knows where you'd be if it weren't for the Counselor."

Mavis jumped out of bed, the sheet falling to the floor. She was a mature woman having just turned thirty but had a youthful strut that still turned heads. She marched across the room and stood in front of the window. "You didn't park in the driveway again, did you?" she asked pulling back the curtain.

"Mavis, if you don't cover up, you're going to start a riot."

"Damn you, Harlan!" she shouted. "You parked in my driveway again! What are the neighbors going to think when they see your corvette out there all night?"

Harlan turned the handle on the door. "Tell them I'm fixing your plumbing," he said and closed the door behind him.

◆◆◆

On the other side of town, the late morning sun found the rain-soaked station wagon parked in the shadows of the abandoned service station. John awoke his body aching from a night of sleeping upright in the driver's seat. He shifted his weight and stretched his legs by leaning back in the seat.

The woman next to him yawned and squinted out the window. "John," she said softly. "There are kids out there staring at us."

John turned to see three young boys standing near the car. He opened the car door and got out. "You boys go find something to do," he said over the top of the car. They did not move. "Go on, now. Get out of here." The tallest glanced at the others but still did not move. "Get the hell out of here!" John shouted. The boys scattered in three directions.

"Jesus, John," said Kara. "Can we at least get curtains for the windows? I feel like I'm in a fishbowl."

"I can do better than that," he said sitting back down. "I'm going to get that job at Bailey's Hardware, and we're going to find us a house. How's that sound to you?"

"It sounds like you're dreaming again."

"Not this time, Karas... not this time. We're going to make it this time."

"I hope you're right, John."

"Right now, I'm going to go see about that job," he said getting back out of the car. "Are you going to be alright?"

"I'll be fine."

"Wish me luck," he said and disappeared around the corner.

Bailey's Hardware had been in the same family since the 1920's. It was an unimpressive building with wood floors and tired, broken displays smelling of old rubber and cigar smoke. Howard Bailey was the last in a line of Baileys who had owned and operated the business. Approaching retirement, Howard was actively looking for someone to operate the store for him.

John opened the front door and closed it behind him. He scanned the sales floor. At the cash register sat an older woman sipping coffee. "Where's Mr. Bailey?" asked John.

She peered over the top of her coffee cup at the man standing near the tools. "He's next door at Moonies," she said. "Who's asking?"

"John Watson," he replied. "Howard asked me to see him about a job."

The old woman sipped her coffee. "John, I think you should know that he's over there talking to Harlan."

"Harlan Steelman?"

"The one and only."

John glanced down at the floor. "That's just great," he muttered and turned to the door. "What are they doing in a bar this time of day?"

"Harlan owns it," she replied without looking up. "Like everything else in town." She set her coffee cup on the counter. "John, you be careful over there. It was a lot of years ago, but you can bet Harlan ain't forgotten."

John turned and studied the old woman. He wasn't quite sure who she was, but it was obvious that she knew him. He opened the door and closed it behind him.

Originally opened as a restaurant, Moonies failed within the first year. It reopened two years later as a quiet neighborhood bar and did well for over a decade until Harlan Steelman became the owner.

John slowly pulled open the front door. It was dark inside. He cautiously stepped inside and closed the door. There were two men sitting at the bar with empty bottles in front of them. "We ain't open yet," announced one of the men.

Mr. Bailey?" asked John.

The two men turned in their seats. One man whispered to the other.

"Is that you, John?" asked Harlan.

"Harlan Steelman?"

"Come on over here, John," said Harlan gulping his beer.

John slowly walked across the floor until he was standing near the men. Silence followed as he studied the two men.

"Want a beer?" asked Harlan draining the last contents of a bottle and opening another.

"No thanks."

"It's on the house."

John turned to Howard Bailey. "You said something about a job."

"Oh yes," said Howard. "That's right."

"I'm here to apply."

"Gee I'm sorry, John," said Howard. "I'm afraid I'm not going to be able to hire you after all, but I'll keep you in mind."

"But you said you needed to hire someone."

"Sorry, John."

John became silent. He turned to Harlan. "You can't let it go, can you Harlan? It's been over and done with for years, and you just can't let it go."

"What the hell are you talking about?" asked Harlan.

"You convinced Mr. Bailey here not to hire me, didn't you? What did you do, Harlan, threaten him?"

"Watch what you say, John," said Harlan. "I was just sitting here having a drink with an old friend. Hell, I didn't even know you were in town."

"Bull shit, Harlan! You're the first to know about anything that happens in this town," said John turning towards the door. "You're still the horse's ass, aren't you Harlan. You haven't changed a bit."

"Hey, I'd be happy to finish what we started way back when," said Harlan with a slur.

"You keep me from getting a job one more time, and we will go a round or two," he said opening the door.

"Anytime!" shouted Harlan. "Anytime!"

It was early in the afternoon when the young man slid down a small hill to the edge of the river. The water was rushing violently from last night's rain. He stared at the currents of grayish murky water swirling by. There would be no swimming today. Carrying a pair of pants and a shirt, Travis followed the riverbank until he came to a small clearing. He stepped down to the water's edge and thrust an arm into the dirty water. It took all his strength to fight the current. He pulled his arm out and stepped away. He then spread the clothes he was carrying on the same rock he had used the day before. He stepped back and stared at the scene. Everything was ready. He scanned the area and walked around a large oak tree.

Travis sat down and leaned against the tree. He closed his eyes and lifted his head, his face bathed in the warm afternoon sunlight. It had been a long, hard winter, and the warm sun felt good on his ashen skin. He smiled as he thought about what he had done. Moments later, his head nodded as he drifted off to sleep.

It was nearly an hour later when Travis was awakened by the sound of laughter. He scrambled to his feet and peeked around the tree. There rushing down the swirling river was a tangled ball of clothing and a young man standing at the rivers edge laughing hysterically.

Travis charged at the man. Melvin looked up. His smiling face turned to shock as he started up the steep bank. As he reached the top, Travis hit him with a flying tackle. The two boys rolled down the hill and into a small clearing. Travis was getting to his feet when Melvin caught him with a right hook that sent him sprawling on his back. He touched his cheek and found it covered with blood. Anger washed over him. He glared at the young man standing over him. "You're going to pay for that," he warned and got to his feet.

The two boys circled one another their fists raised in a fighting posture. Suddenly, Melvin reached out and pushed Travis sending him back-stepping. Melvin turned and ran with Travis close behind.

Travis leaped forward and caught Melvin by the ankles. The two boys fell and began rolling on the ground. They reached the top of the bank and fell over the edge gathering speed as they rolled towards the water. The rain-swollen river was nearly twelve inches higher than normal, and the two boys plunged into the raging river disappearing under the surface. The swirling currents grabbed the boys and pulled them to the center of the river. They both surfaced gasping for air.

"I can't swim!" shouted Melvin. He was less than ten feet away. Travis began to swim towards the boy. He thrashed his arms against the violent currents until he was within an arm's length of Melvin. Travis extended his hand. "Grab hold!" he shouted. Melvin stretched his hand until his fingers were nearly touching those of Travis, but the angry river would not allow it. The boys were pulled under their bodies spinning and tumbling out of control racing down the river for what seemed like an eternity.

Suddenly, a sharp current spun Travis around. He felt himself bump into something. It had to be Melvin. By now, his lungs were on fire. He reached out and grabbed him by the arm. With a firm grip on the boy's arm, Travis kicked his way to the surface.

Then, miraculously, they broke the surface only six feet from the river's edge. Their lungs exploded as they gasped for air. The currents were less violent in this part of the river, but they were being swept down river at a rapid pace.

Travis pricked his ears. He heard something in the distance. "Are you alright?" he shouted.

"I'm fine," said Melvin.

"What's that noise?"

Melvin paused. "Oh my God!" he shouted. "That's a waterfall! We're heading for a waterfall! We've got to get out of here!"

For a moment, Travis stared down the river as if he could see the impending danger. He gripped Melvin's arm even tighter and started kicking towards the riverbank. He fought against the currents until he was within inches of reaching the soft dirt. He dropped his feet down and found the muddy river bottom. He tried digging his toes in the mud but with no success. He reached for a tree root that protruded from the riverbank, but it snapped from the weight.

Another strong current sweeping down the river at an even faster pace caught them. They brushed against the riverbank hitting rocks and branches. They started to spin with the current both of them reaching for anything to slow their movement.

The falls was getting close. Travis could hear the roar of water cascading over the edge. He reached for a branch, but it was unattached and simply followed them down the river. Travis released it and turned to look ahead.

There it was. The falls was straight ahead. He had seconds to do something. He was near exhaustion but summoned enough energy to make one last try. He gripped Melvin's arm until his nails pierced the skin. He kicked towards the riverbank hoping to snare a large rock that was only a few feet from the falls.

"Grab my neck!" he shouted at Melvin as he released his grip on Melvin's arm. He now had the use of both hands. The swirling motion of the river stopped now as the depth of the water became much shallower, but the speed of the current was now faster than ever.

Travis wiped the water from his eyes. He held both arms out of the water with his hands ready to grab the rock. His temple throbbed as his heart pounded in his chest. There was no room for failure this time. It had to be perfect. He had no idea how much of a drop there was over the edge and if there was a deep pool of water waiting at the bottom or piles of huge rocks as was often the case.

The rock was only a few feet away. They were moving even faster now. Travis tensed his body. He dug his heels into the soft mud. He reached and encircled the rock like a lasso. Their bodies sped past the rock and then jolted to a stop.

Travis hung on as tightly as he could. The rock was slippery, but he held tight. Their bodies were now waving in the current like a giant flag. Melvin was now holding onto his waist. He struggled against the current to plant his feet on the river bottom.

Travis strained to hold on. His muscles ached, but he fought to hold his grip. Melvin found the river bottom. He tried to dig his toes into the soft mud but slipped and soon found himself being sucked downstream again.

This sudden movement caused a jolt for Travis who by now was slowly losing his grip. Travis let go of the rock. He scratched at it until his fingers bled. They drifted slowly from the rock gathering speed as they headed for the falls. They were inches from the riverbank and the water was shallow, but they were completely exhausted. They swirled, lifelessly, towards the falls the water roaring in celebration of its victory.

As they reached the crest of the falls, two massive dark hands reached down and grabbed the two boys by the shirts. They were dragged out of the water, up the riverbank, and dropped on the ground.

Travis lay on his back desperately gasping for air. He opened his eyes and stared up at the monster towering over him. He was nearly seven feet tall with massive arms and chest. His dirty black hair fell down his back, his beard hiding all but two glaring red eyes.

"Who are you?" asked Travis sitting up. The man said nothing. Travis turned to Melvin who was staring at the man with his mouth open. "Well, I don't know who you are, but you sure saved our asses."

The big man stared at Travis and then turned to Melvin. Saliva dripped from his open mouth. His clothes were made from animal skins and he wore no shoes. He stepped over the two boys and walked away.

"Hey, mister," shouted Travis. "What's your name?"

"Never mind," said Melvin touching his arm.

"Why?" asked Travis.

"He won't say anything."

"Why not?"

"He's known as Lone Wolf, and they say he can't speak. At least, nobody has ever heard him speak."

"Where does he live?"

"Somewhere out there," said Melvin pointing at the woods.

"What do you mean somewhere out there?"

"I mean he lives out there in the forest. No one knows where, but according to legend, he lives with the wolves. Nobody really knows his real name."

Travis stared at the man as he disappeared into the woods. "Do you believe that shit?"

"What shit?" asked Melvin.

"Do you believe he lives with the wolves?"

"Why not?" Melvin asked. "He looks like an animal himself."

Travis got to his feet. He stared down at Melvin. "Are you alright?" he asked holding out a hand.

"Yeah, I'm okay," he said taking his hand. "Except, maybe, where you dug your nails in my arm. Ever thought about trimming those things back?"

Travis stared into the woods. "Have you ever seen that Lone Wolf before?"

"He's been to town a couple times," said Melvin brushing dirt from his clothes.

"What does he live in?"

"They say he lives in a tarpaper shack somewhere out there."

"Come on," said Travis starting for the woods. "Let's go find out where he lives."

Melvin paused. He turned to the woods and then back to Travis. "I don't think so," he said brushing himself again.

"Why not?"

Lone Wolf doesn't like people, and he sure doesn't like people who snoop around where he lives."

"You know he doesn't hate us," said Travis. "If he did, he sure wouldn't have saved our butts. Now, come on."

"There's something else you don't know about Lone Wolf," said Melvin with a soft voice.

"And what's that?" asked Travis.

Melvin paused. He scanned the area and then turned back to Travis. "They say that he not only lives with the wolves, he actually turns into one."

"What?"

"I'm just telling you what they say."

"You mean like a Werewolf? He turns into a Werewolf?"

"No, nothing like that," said Melvin. "He turns into a wolf. You know, the four-legged kind."

"Did anybody ever see him do it?"

"No white people ever did," said Melvin. "Other Indians say they've seen him do it."

"Other Indians. You mean Lone Wolf is a real live Indian?"

"What the hell did you think he was?"

"I don't know. I ain't never seen a real Indian before."

"Jesus, where have you been? There's a whole tribe of 'em over by Steam Corners."

"Come on," said Travis starting towards the woods. "Let's go see for ourselves."

"Okay, but I don't like it," said Melvin following behind.

"Besides, I owe you one," said Travis.

"You owe me what?"

"I owe you for that lucky punch you gave me," he said rubbing his cheek.

"That wasn't lucky."

"What do you call it?"

"I call it a great punch."

"You can call it whatever you want, but I owe you one," said Travis heading deep into the woods.

The two boys picked their way through the thick underbrush pushing deeper into the forest. Oak and maple trees reached proudly and maKaratically into the sky their leaves forming a canopy that let only the smallest amount of light to reach the ground below.

"I don't like this," said Melvin leaning against a tree.

Travis studied the area. "Why do you say that?" he asked.

"It's so dark and quiet around here," said Melvin. "Hell, you can't even hear any birds I have never been anyplace where there are no birds. Something isn't right around here. I can feel it."

Travis paused. "You're right about one thing. There are no birds around. Wonder why?"

"I don't know, but I get the feeling they're smarter than we are," said Melvin. "Now, let's get the hell out of here."

Travis slowly scanned the area. "There it is," he said pointing in the distance.

"There what is?" asked Melvin peering into the woods.

"The tarpaper shack that Lone Wolf lives in," said Travis. "Let's go."

"Oh Christ," said Melvin. "I don't think this is such a good idea."

Travis turned and stared at Melvin. "How could someone pack a punch like you do and be scared of a shack in the woods?"

"It's not the shack I'm worried about," he replied falling into step.

The trees in that part of the forest were nearly side-by-side their foliage creating an umbrella that seemed to hide that part of the world. The scant light that filtered through the leaves cast a greenish hue on the ground below. There was no wind. The leaves hung motionlessly as if petrified. In spite of the near absence of light and deep layers of fallen leaves, thick vine-like undergrowth spread across the forest floor like so many entangled serpents.

Travis and Melvin stopped a few feet from the crudely constructed building. The walls and roof were covered with tarpaper and the only opening was a doorway without a door.

"I don't like this," said Melvin. "There's something evil about this place."

"Come on," said Travis. "Let's see if your Mr. Lone Wolf is home."

"Travis," said Melvin grabbing him by the arm. "Somebody is watching us!"

Travis jumped. "Will you stop it? You nearly scared me to death."

"I'm telling you someone is watching us," said Melvin. "The hairs on the back of my neck are standing straight up."

Travis paused. He glanced at the structure and then back at Melvin. "You wait here," he said starting for the open doorway. "I'm going to check the place out."

"Not a problem," said Melvin. "I'm as close to that place as I want to get."

Travis walked slowly to the doorway and cautiously stepped inside. It was a small building not much larger than a bedroom. It was dark inside, but Travis could see that at one end a bed had been fashioned from straw and at the other end was a bench about waist high that ran the length of the wall. There was no food or cooking utensils, yet there was a stench of rotting flesh that filled the air.

"What do you see?" shouted Melvin.

"Nothing," Travis replied.

"Well then, let's go," Melvin suggested.

Travis walked to the back of the shack. He bent down in the dark. Lying in one corner was a heap of tattered and dirty clothing. He picked through the foul-smelling clothes and dropped them on the bed of straw. Hidden under the pile of clothes was a tree branch about the size of a baseball bat. Travis carefully picked it up and carried it to the light of the doorway. He rolled it over in his hands. It was covered with deep punctures.

"What did you find in there?" asked Melvin.

"I don't know," said Travis. "It looks like some animal has been chewing on this wood."

"That means just one thing to me," said Melvin.

"What's that?"

"It's time to go."

Travis reared his head. "I hear something," he whispered.

"Oh Christ!"

"Something's moving in the leaves."

Melvin searched the area. "Wolf!" he cried. "I see a wolf!"

"Where?"

"Over there," said Melvin pointing in the distance.

Travis became perfectly still. He searched the area. "Are you sure it was a wolf?" he asked with a hushed voice.

"It was gray with a long tail and red eyes! Is that good enough?"

Travis glanced up at the fading sunlight. It's getting late, not much daylight left," he said. "Let's get out of here!"

CHAPTER 4

Alone woman walked down Main Street carrying a bag of groceries. She turned down an unpaved alley that passed next to Harry Miller's Gas Station. She turned the corner that led to the back of the abandoned building and stopped in front of a parked station wagon. She set the bag on the hood and turned to lean against the car. It had been a long walk and she needed a moment to catch her breath. Kara glanced up at the blue sky as she wiped her forehead. The afternoon sun was hot. She unfastened the top buttons of her blouse and turned to face the sun. Her soft white skin tingled in the bright sunshine. She kicked off one of her shoes and bent down to remove a stone.

Kara heard a car turn down the alley its exhaust sounding like distant thunder. A black corvette came to an abrupt stop just in front of her the dust rising and softly settling on the lacquer finish.

A tall young man stepped from the car and walked around to the other side. "How are you, Kara?" he asked leaning against the car.

"I wondered when you'd be coming around here," she said.

"The years have been kind to you, girl," he said with a smile. "I swear you look better now than you did back then."

Kara smiled. She slowly bent over to slip on her shoe her breasts swaying inside her open blouse. Harlan felt the blood pounding through his veins as he stared. He smiled as he watched her slowly stand up.

"Sorry," she said fastening the buttons.

"My, my, my," he said. "That's one lucky guy."

"Who's a lucky guy?"

"John," Harlan replied. "Who else?"

Kara glanced at the station wagon, her smiled disappeared. "You call this lucky?" Silence followed. "You hadn't ought to be here," she said. "John should be here any time."

"Ever been for a ride in a corvette?"

Kara smiled. "Can't say as I have," she replied.

"Come on. Let's go for a quick spin."

Kara paused. "I can't."

"Why not?"

"John should be home, and I ain't fixed him his dinner."

"We'll only be gone for a minute. You'll be back long before John gets here."

Kara began to slide her wedding ring up and down on her finger. "Sure is a pretty car," she said.

Harlan stared at her as she played with her ring. "Wait 'til you see how fast she can go," he said as if aroused from a trance.

Kara paused. "No, I can't," she said. "Maybe, some other day."

"Suit yourself," said Harlan walking around to the driver's side. "By the way, if you need a job, just let me know."

"Well, as a matter of fact, we, or rather, John needs one," she said.

"I'm not talking about John," said Harlan opening the door of his car. "I'm talking about a job for you. My dad needs someone to cook for him."

"Does he still live on the ranch?"

"Still there," said Harlan getting into his car. "What do you say?"

"I don't know," she said reaching for her groceries. "I'll have to talk it over with John.

Harlan started the engine. He revved it several times and let it idle. "Sure was nice seeing you again, Kara," he said looking out the window. "You think about that job."

"I will," she replied picking up the groceries.

Harlan stared at her for several moments and then slowly eased the car away.

It was nearly six o'clock when John slipped into the driver's seat of the car. Kara had just finished making sandwiches.

"Hungry?" she asked.

"Starved," he said taking a bite of food. "How was your day?"

"It was alright," she replied pouring him a glass of water. "Did you find a job?"

"Not even close," he said taking the glass. "It's like I have some kind of disease. Everyone turns me down, and the thing about it is they won't even look me in the eye when they do it." John took a sip of water and set down the glass. "Of course, I know why all this is happening."

Kara bit into her sandwich. "Why is that?"

"It's that God damn Harlan, and you know it. He's got everyone in this town wrapped around his little finger. I never dreamed that after all these years he would be like this."

"Do you think he has spread the word not to hire you?"

"I'm sure of it. Even my old friends are acting strange."

Kara set her sandwich on the dashboard and wiped her mouth. "John, maybe we should get out of here. Maybe, we should try a new start in another town."

"Just because of Harlan Steelman? Not on your life. I won't let the likes of him run me out of town. I'll find a job. You'll see."

"Harlan was here," she said softly.

John stopped chewing. He turned in his seat. "When was he here?" he snapped.

"A short while ago."

"What did he want?"

"Nothing much," she replied. "He just wanted to say hello."

"I don't like that bastard coming around here. Did he try anything?"

"Come on, John," she said. "You don't think that after all these years he's going to come around here and try anything, do you?"

"You must not know Harlan Steelman as well as I thought you did."

"He offered me a job."

"Who did?"

"Harlan, who else?'

"Doing what?"

"Cookin' for his daddy."

"Ain't no way in the world you're working for Harlan Steelman!" John shouted.

"I wouldn't be working for Harlan," she said turning in her seat. "I'd be working for his dad."

"You'd still be working for the Steelmans, and I don't like that."

"We need the money, John," she said. "Besides, it would only be for a short while. I would quit when you get a job."

John became silent. He took another bite from his sandwich. "That son of a bitch has been a pain in my ass for all my life."

"How would you get out there?" asked John. "The Steelman ranch is nearly a half mile out of town."

"I can walk," she replied. "I used to do it years ago." John turned in her direction. Kara turned back and took a bite of her sandwich. "Sorry," she said softly. "So, what do you think? Can I get the job?"

John paused. He searched her eyes for some kind of sign. I suppose so. It all don't matter much anyhow," said John his face turning to a smile. "I plan on finding a job tomorrow. There's got to be someone in this town who isn't owned by Harlan Steelman. Tomorrow, I will find someone who will give me a job even if I have to wash dishes."

◆◆◆

The next morning brought a gray overcast sky with clouds that seemed to touch the earth. Travis rounded the corner onto Main Street. He had agreed to meet Melvin by nine o'clock, and it was already past ten. He turned a corner at another side street and walked two blocks until he was standing at the base of the American flag in front of the Post Office.

"Where have you been, asshole?" said Melvin.

Travis searched the area. "Where are you?"

"Over here, dumb ass," said Melvin getting up from a park bench. "I can't believe I waited all this time so that I can go tramping in the woods again."

"I just want to talk with this Lone Wolf guy," said Travis starting down the street.

"Maybe, you didn't understand something," said Melvin falling in step. "What you heard yesterday and what I saw was not just any old wolf. That was your Lone Wolf, and when Lone Wolf isn't running through the woods on all fours, he still isn't the kind to be asking two young idiots like us in for tea. He really does frown on people snooping around his place."

The two boys crossed over the railroad tracks and started down a country road that led out of town. "I just want to talk with him," said Travis. "I don't think he's the monster you say he is."

"And I'm just fool enough to go with you," said Melvin. "You know this guy eats kids like us for lunch."

"You have nothing to worry about," said Travis.

"Why?"

"He wouldn't eat anything as ugly as you," he said with a smile.

Melvin turned and stared at the young man strutting beside him. He saw the smile on Travis' face. "Smart ass," he uttered.

They jumped a fence and started across a field. "What are you doing Saturday night?" asked Melvin.

"Are you asking me out?"

"No, asshole," said Melvin. "I'm asking you to help me out. The only way Linda Sue's mother will let me take her out is on a double date, and that's where you come in."

"Who is Linda Sue?"

"Just the most beautiful girl in the world and my future wife."

"Does she have big ones?"

"What?"

"You know, sweater meat. Does she have big hooters?"

"Jesus, you're talking about the girl I love," said Melvin. "That's the kind of question you ask a guy about some tramp that he's dating just to get some. A guy doesn't mind talking about a chick like that, but this is different. Linda Sue is a goddess. She's the woman of my dreams. She's the woman I plan to marry and raise a family with."

"Well, does she?"

Melvin smiled. "Yeah, they aren't bad."

"Well, we've got one problem. I don't have a girl to take."

"That's all been taken care of," said Melvin. "We've got you lined up with Linda's best friend, Sara. You talk about big ones. Have you ever known a girl by the name of Sara who didn't have big ones?"

Travis bowed his head. "I don't know about this."

"What do you mean?"

"What if she's ugly?"

"I've seen her. She's really cute. Besides, if you don't like her, you can leave early. I'll take her home."

"I don't know," said Travis. "I've never been on a date before."

"How old are you?"

"Sixteen. Kind of."

"What does that mean?'

"I'll be sixteen in a few days."

"Then it's time you entered the adult world," said Melvin with his head held high. "It's time you grabbed a little female flesh. You might even get your wick wet."

Travis paled. "I couldn't do that," he said nervously. "I don't even know the girl."

"Hey, what you do in the backseat is no concern of mine," said Melvin. "Don't worry. There's no way I would ever glance back there. I'd be too afraid of seeing you without clothes."

"I've never been on a date before," said Travis. "What do I do? What am I suppose to talk about?"

"I'm not real sure," said Melvin. "I just know you're supposed to try to get to first base, and if you make it there you try for second. Of course, the whole idea is to make it to home plate."

"What's at home plate?"

"You know."

Travis paused. "No, I don't know."

"Ah, come on," said Melvin. "Everyone knows where home plate is.'

"Well, I don't," said Travis turning in his direction.

"It's getting laid, you dumb ass," said Melvin. "It's called getting some nooky."

"What makes you such an expert?" asked Travis. "You're the same age as me."

"I just know about these things," he said. "I've been around. Besides, my folks have a sex manual hidden behind the other regular books. It tells about everything. It even has drawings."

"What kind of drawings?"

"It has drawings of women's breasts and other things."

"What other things?"

"You know."

"No, I don't know. What things?"

"You know, women's things. Drawings of women with their legs spread, and you can see everything. I'll bet you never even seen a picture of a naked woman."

"Yes, I have."

"Where did you see it?"

"National Geographic. They got lots of pictures in there."

"That don't count."

"Why not?"

"Those people run around without clothes all the time. It's not the same."

"I guess I don't understand."

Melvin stopped and turned to Travis. "Seeing some young blond-haired, blue-eyed babe take her clothes off in front of you is far better than seeing some old chick from Africa. Besides, their tits are saggy."

"Why is that?"

"They don't wear no bras. Something happens to 'em. All I know is they got tits that point at their shoe tops, that is if they wore shoes." They turned and started for the woods. "So, what do you think? Do you want to double date this Saturday?"

Travis paused. "Yeah, I'll go but tell me one thing. Do I kiss her good night?"

"Of course, you kiss her," said Melvin. "She owes you that. You show her a good time, and she owes you that much. Actually, you should get to feel her up a couple times. That's the least she can do for you."

Travis turned with a puzzled look. "Jesus, I don't even think I have the nerve to kiss her."

Melvin turned to his friend. "You sure got a lot to learn," he said shaking his head.

The two boys jumped another fence and were now at the edge of the forest. They turned and looked at each other and without saying a word began a slow march.

The forest closed in on them like a shroud. There was a dank wetness in the air and the light grew darker with each step. Silence fell on the forest like an open grave. The two boys slowed to a cautious crawl their footfalls crashing in the amber leaves of last year's autumn.

"Jesus, this place is scary," said Melvin his head moving in all directions.

"It's almost as if the forest is alive," said Travis, "and it knows we're here."

They both stopped and scanned the woods. "It feels like someone is watching us," said Melvin.

"There it is!" shouted Travis pointing in the woods.

Melvin jumped. "There what is?"

"Lone Wolf's shack."

Melvin strained to see. "I don't think I want to meet Lone Wolf again," he said turning around. " I think we wore out our welcome the first day we met him."

Travis grabbed his arm. "Come on," he whispered. "Let's go see the wolf man."

"I wish you wouldn't put it that way," said Melvin.

The two boys started for the shack their every step echoing throughout the forest. They stopped just outside the open door both searching the area.

"This place is scary," said Melvin. "It's too damn quiet."

"Well, the one thing about it is nobody is going to sneak up on you," said Travis. "You'd hear 'em coming for a mile."

"I still don't like it," said Melvin.

"Quit your whining," said Travis starting for the door. "Let's go see if anybody is home."

"Have you always had this death wish?" he asked following behind.

The two boys cautiously stepped inside and looked around. There was a stench in the room like rotting flesh. Travis walked to the back of the room and knelt down. In the dark, he searched through the straw for the tattered clothes that just yesterday were lying in a heap.

"Wonder what happened to the nasty smelling clothes that were here yesterday," said Travis standing up.

"I don't know, and I don't care," said Melvin. "I just know it's time to get out of here."

"Well, somebody has been here," said Travis. "Somebody came and took those clothes, and if they are wearing them now, where were they yesterday without any clothes on?"

Melvin jumped. "I hear something," he whispered grabbing his friend's arm.

The two boys froze. "What did you hear?" asked Travis.

"I'm not sure," he replied. "It sounded like someone in the leaves."

They paused as they listened. "Come on," said Travis. "Let's go take a look." Travis crept outside with Melvin close behind. They stopped just outside the door and scanned the area.

"See anything?"

"No, how 'bout you?"

From inside the small shack came a deep, thunderous voice. "What you doing here?"

The two boys jumped. They spun around to see a nearly seven-foot tall Indian standing in the doorway of the building they had just left. "Lone Wolf!" shouted Travis.

"My name not Lone Wolf," he said his eyebrows furrowed with anger.

"What is your name?" blurted Travis with a wide-eyed stare.

"You go now," he said pointing into the distance.

"Come on," said Melvin. "Let's get out of here."

"One more question," said Travis. "Why did you save our lives yesterday? Was it because you like us for some reason?"

"Your bloated carcasses attract bear. That no good."

Melvin leaned over and whispered to Travis. "So much for a new friend in our lives. Let's go."

"One more question," blurted Travis.

"You ask too many questions," said Lone Wolf.

"A minute ago you weren't anywhere near here, and then all of a sudden you appear in your doorway. No matter where you walk out here, anybody can hear you, and yet we heard nothing. How can you explain that?"

Lone Wolf stood straight. A faint smile appeared on his face.

Travis glanced at Melvin and then back at Lone Wolf. "Some say you can turn into a wolf. Is that true?"

Lone Wolf said nothing. He brushed the long, dark hair from his face, turned, and reentered his home. He picked up the limp body of a freshly killed rabbit and dropped it on the wooden table. His hand moved swiftly across his body producing a hunting knife over ten inches long. Travis and Melvin inched their way to the doorway and watched as the huge man began to skin the animal. Within seconds, he peeled the fur from the animal and threw it into the corner.

Lone Wolf walked back outside and fell to his knees a few feet from the shack. He broke small branches and dropped them into a pile on the ground. He reached into a pocket and pulled out a match. Snapping it with his thumbnail, it roared to life.

"I thought you guys used the sun or something," said Travis.

Lone Wolf turned and stared, his match still lit. "Never did learn that kind of stuff," he said setting leaves on fire. "Besides, much easier with match."

The two boys smiled at each other. Not only was this man human, but he had a sense of humor as well.

"So, are you going to tell us or not?" asked Travis.

"Tell you what?" Lone Wolf asked getting to his feet.

"Your name. What's your real name?"

The big man walked over and picked up the skinned, bloody rabbit. He stuck a small branch through the animal and fashioned a stand from two sticks to hold the makeshift spit. He broke several small branches into pieces and tossed them on the fire. Burning ashes rose with the smoke and settled on the meat.

"We'll tell you our names," said Travis. "My name is Travis, and this is Melvin. So, what's yours? Must be Running Bear or something like that."

"Why you want to know?" asked Lone Wolf sitting on a fallen tree near his fire.

"Why not?" asked Melvin. "We've never met a real live Indian. We're just curious, that's all."

All eyes watched as Lone Wolf slowly turned the wooden spit over the dancing flames. "You forgot to gut that animal," said Melvin. "You're cooking the meat with its organs still inside."

"No waste food," said Lone Wolf still staring at the animal.

Melvin turned to Travis and then back to Lone Wolf. "What do you mean by no waste food?"

Lone Wolf stopped turning the spit. He looked up at Melvin. "Eat all rabbit."

"You're not going to eat the guts too, are you?" he asked.

"That best part," Lone Wolf replied.

Melvin grimaced. "That's sick," he said.

"What sick?"

"Eating innards."

"Which ones?"

"Which ones what?"

"Which innards sick?"

"All of them," said Melvin. "My God, man, are you telling me you like eating all of the internal organs of small animals?"

"No like intestines," said Lone Wolf with a frown. "Eat anyway."

"Oh, my God," said Melvin turning to Travis. He stared at his friend and said nothing.

Travis cleared his throat. "So, is it true what they say about your turning into a Lone Wolf?"

Lone Wolf gathered some sticks lying nearby and carefully dropped them into the fire. Lit ashes swirled into the air and settled on the cooking meat. "What you think?" he asked without looking up.

"I think it's true," said Travis without hesitation.

"What make you think that?"

Travis paused. He studied the man who was tending to his dinner. "When we first got here, there was no one around besides us, then all of a sudden you appeared. There's no way you could have sneaked up on us without our hearing you." Lone Wolf said nothing. "Well, how do you explain it?"

"Look at me," said Lone Wolf looking up. "Me Indian. We good at sneaking."

Suddenly, he got to his feet towering over the two boys. "Now time for you to go," he said pointing into the forest. "It time to eat food and want to be alone."

"Not a problem," said Travis getting to his feet. "If you're about to eat a rabbit's guts then it's time for me to go, but you never did answer my question."

"What that?"

"What's your real name? Running water, right?"

The big man stared at the boys and then pointed once again. "Go!" he shouted, and the two boys disappeared into the woods.

◆◆◆

On the other side of town a young woman slowly walked alongside of County Road 109. A soft rain began to fall but there was no turning back. She turned onto an unpaved drive that led to one of the largest farms in the state. For generations, the Steelmans owned some of the most fertile land in that part of the country, and until recently, every year was another record setting harvest.

It had been a lifelong dream of Nolan Steelman to retire and pass the operation of the farm onto his two sons. For the past fifty years he had cared for and tended the sprawling farm having reared a family from the generous yields that were harvested each year.

For nearly all his life, Nolan Steeman had been an important part of the community. Everyone knew that no one with a problem was ever turned away by Nolan Steelman, but all that changed. A major heart attack and the loss of his wife had left Nolan a recluse.

Kara stopped just in front of the walk that led to the massive front porch. It was a large two-story white farmhouse with black shutters. The barn and out buildings spread out like a small village, but something was wrong. There was a feeling of death in the air. Weeds grew where once there were none. Peeling white paint speckled the ground like freshly fallen snow. A small tree had fallen in the front yard partially hidden by the weeds.

Kara stepped onto the porch her feet leaving prints in the thick dust and lightly tapped on the eight-foot high front door. She heard a faint voice directing her to come inside.

Kara slowly opened the door letting the morning light pour into the dark interior. A fog of dust particles floated in and out of the light. She squinted as she peered into the darkness. Smells of rotting wood and stale cigarette smoke rushed from the room.

"Who are you and what do you want?" someone asked from the darkness.

Kara stepped to the edge of the light and studied the outline of a man sitting in an easy chair. The red glow from a cigarette seemed to hover near the chair. "My name is Kara Watson, and I'm here to see about the job," she said softly.

Silence fell on the room. The old man reached over and turned on a lamp. The dim glow from a 25-watt bulb did little to illuminate the room. Kara quickly glanced around the room. The walls were covered with faded flower print wallpaper with dark stain woodwork. Her eyes fell on an old man sitting in a torn cloth chair. He reached over and snubbed out his cigarette and quickly lit another.

"How did you know there was a job opening?" he asked.

"Your son, Harlan told me," she replied still standing in the open doorway.

The old man leaned forward as he studied the young woman. "I only knew one Kara my whole life," he said squinting to see. "You ain't Hal Stewart's daughter, are you?"

"That's me," she said taking a step forward.

"Oh, my God! It is you! Come on in and sit down," he said pointing at the sofa. He was an old man with snow-white hair and beard. His face was weatherworn with eyes that drooped. He wore dark clothes with a dark gray sweater, and he wore a wicked frown that seemed to be etched in his face.

Kara sat down on the side next to the old man. "Nothing bad happened to your cook, I hope."

"I fired the dumb ass woman!" he shouted. He pounded his fist on the arm of his chair knocking ashes to the floor. "She wouldn't fix what I wanted. God, I hated that woman."

"What was it that you wanted her to cook?" she asked.

"I wanted fried eggs and bacon for breakfast and fried potatoes and sausage for dinner. You know, the good stuff. She kept feeding me oatmeal and salads and all that healthy stuff. I warned her, by God. I warned her that I would fire her if she didn't cook what I wanted."

"Sounds like she was only doing it for your own good," said Kara. "They say you'll live a lot longer if you eat right."

"Kara, I'm in my sixties now. How long do you think I'm going to live? When you get to be my age you might as well eat what you want and enjoy life. Don't you agree?"

"Well, I suppose…"

"So, what can I do for you?"

"The job," said Kara. "I'm interested in the job."

"Oh yes, the job," he said inhaling his cigarette. He paused for a moment. "You used to come around here years ago, didn't you?"

"Yes, I used to date Harlan."

"Now, I remember," said Nolan. "God, it's great seeing you again. Yes, indeed. You always were a pretty one. He sure let a good one get away. Seems to me you never were completely sold on Harlan. Weren't you dating someone else as well?"

Kara glanced away. "I was dating John Watson too," she said softly.

"Oh yeah. That's right," he said smiling. "I remember that name. God, how Harlan hated John Watson. I swear if I hadn't stepped in, he'd have killed that man. Wonder what ever happened to him."

"I married him," she said looking up.

"You married him! Oh, my God! Does Harlan know about this?"

"Yes, he knows."

"You married John Watson," he said looking away. He paused as he thought for a moment. "You know, I don't know whether to congratulate you or kick you out of here. Harlan turned mean after he lost you. I never knew at the time just why he got that way, but in time I pieced things together from things he said. It just seemed like he wanted to take it out on everyone he ever knew. To this day I don't know whether it was because he lost you or lost to John."

"I don't understand," said Kara.

"Harlan is very competitive. He don't like to lose to nobody, and you were the biggest prize of all. Oh, don't get me wrong. I know he loved you. Fact is, I think he still does. It's just he can't stand to lose especially a prize rose like you."

"Well, thank you, Mr.Steelman."

"Call me Nolan," he said as he smothered his cigarette in the ashtray. "Ain't no need to be so formal. Hell, if things had gone a little differently, you might be calling me your father-in-law."

Kara gave a polite smile.

"You did the right thing, you know. He's an evil man, now," said Nolan lighting another cigarette. "I can say it because I'm his father, but I can tell you he ain't no good. He lives here with me. He's supposed to be running the farm, but you can see he's just running it into the ground." Nolan expelled a cloud of smoke into the room. "I can't stand to see what he's doing to this place, but what can I do? I'm too old, and my old ticker is just about worn out."

Kara said nothing. Nolan leaned forward. "So, tell me about yourself. How's it going with you?"

"Everything is fine," she said looking down at the floor.

"No, it's not," said Nolan.

Kara looked up. There was a look of sadness in her eyes. "What?" she asked.

"I maybe old and I might not be too smart, but I know people, and you've got troubles," said the old man.

Kara turned away. She paused for a moment and then turned back with a smile. "We're just having a little financial setback right now. That's all."

Nolan said nothing. He waited as if he expected her to continue. "Can you start next Monday morning about eight?" he asked leaning back in his chair.

"I'll be here," she said getting to her feet. She walked across the living room and stood in the open doorway. "I'll see you in a couple days, Mr. Steelman."

The old man leaned forward. "You mind yourself around Harlan," he said with an ominous voice. "He's not to be trusted."

Kara stared at the old man. It seemed strange to hear a man speak of his own son in such a manner. "I'll be careful," she said and closed the door.

◆◆◆

It was Saturday night, and the little town of Bear Creek was turning out for the event of the year. Every third weekend in June, the downtown area was blocked off and a travelling carnival set up rides and games spreading down Main Street from the hardware store to the school.

Travis was sitting in the backseat of the car. He pushed his shirttail into pants and ran his fingers through his hair. "Where's pop?" he asked leaning over to look into the rearview mirror.

"Looking for a job," said his mother without turning around.

"Why is he looking for a job on a Saturday?" asked Travis. "Nobody hires on a Saturday."

"I don't think your dad wants me to get a job," she said. "I think he's trying to find one before Monday so I won't have to go."

"Why?" asked Travis leaning back in the seat. "What makes the difference who earns the money?"

Kara turned and stared out the window. "Your father is a man," she said softly. "Any man worth anything at all has more pride than to let his wife support him." She turned in her seat. "Your father is just trying to restore his pride. That's all. Besides, I don't think he wants me working for the Steelmans."

Travis paused. "Why? What's wrong with the Steelmans?"

His mother turned to the window. "It's something that happened a long time ago. It's something that should never have happened."

Travis stared at his mother half expecting an explanation. "My friend's name is Steelman. Melvin Steelman. In fact, he's the one I'm going with tonight."

Kara turned in her seat to face her son. "You be careful around that boy. You be careful around any Steelman. They're rich and powerful, and they take whatever they want."

Travis said nothing. There was something in his mother's voice he had never before heard.

"God, I'm so nervous," he said twisting in his seat. "This is my first date, and I really don't know what to do."

"You'll be fine," said his mother with a smile. "Just be nice to her. All girls like to have someone treat 'em nice. I guess that's one thing guys never seem to understand. It ain't money that we want or big houses and things; it's just someone to treat us like a lady. That's all. You open the door for her and tell her how pretty she is, and you won't have no problems." She paused and smiled at her son. Her eyes glowed as the memories washed over her. "Doesn't seem possible that you're going out on a date. You're so young."

A red convertible came to a stop next to the station wagon. Travis peered out the back window. He could see Melvin at the wheel and a girl in the front seat and one in the back. He paused as he studied his date. She leaned slightly forward and quickly shook her head sending her long flowing blond hair cascading down back. "Got to go," he said getting out of the car.

"Have fun," said his mother.

The young man walked over to the car and stood by the door. "This is my friend, Linda Sue," said Melvin pointing at the girl next to him. He then turned to the girl in the backseat. "This is Sara."

Travis turned and smiled at the girl. "Hi," he blurted.

"Hi," she returned as she shifted to one side of the seat. She shyly glanced down and then back to the young man her hair falling gently into her blue eyes.

"I told you she was a beauty," said Melvin. "Now, get in, so we can get going."

Linda pulled her seat forward as Travis stepped into the backseat. His foot caught the doorsill, and he fell forward his head landing in Sara's lap. "Oh, my God!" he exclaimed his head still resting on her legs and his feet dangling out the door.

Sara stared down at the young man her hands in the air. "Glad to meet you," she said with a smile.

Melvin turned in his seat. "Atta boy," he said turning back around. "Go get 'em, Tiger."

Travis scrambled to his feet. "I feel so bad about this," he said taking his place at the far end of the seat. "I'm so sorry."

"What was that you were telling me about this being your first date?" asked Melvin slowly driving away. "Anybody as suave as you has been around. Don't kid me."

Travis glanced at his date and then turned away. She was wearing a long, white summer dress, and her blue eyes seemed to glow against her soft fair skin. "I really am sorry," he said softly. "I'm not usually this clumsy. Really, I'm not."

"It's okay," she said sitting back in her seat.

Travis glanced at the Melvin who was smiling at him in the rearview mirror. "My name is Travis," he said extending his hand.

"I'm Sara," she said shaking his hand.

"Sara. That name sounds familiar," said Travis.

Sara rhymes with Tara. You know, Gone with the Wind," she said. Travis looked puzzled. "You know. Tara was the plantation in the movie, Gone with the Wind."

"Gone with the Wind?" he questioned. "Never heard of it. I just meant that I once had a lizard named Sara."

"Oh," she said turning away. She turned with a puzzled look. "You never heard of Gone with the Wind?"

Travis looked away. "We don't get to see many movies," he said.

"Actually I've never seen the movie either," she said. "It was made a long time ago, but I did read the book. Did you ever read the book?"

"No."

"Oh."

"I read Tom Sawyer last summer. Have you ever read that one?"

"Everybody has read Tom Sawyer."

"Not my dad," blurted Travis. "Of course, I'm not real sure he can read. Never really did see him read anything. Seen him looking at a map before, but I'm not real sure you need to read to figure one of them out."

"What does your father do?"

"Nothing. He's unemployed right now."

"Oh," said Sara turning away. "Where are you living?"

"In that car back there."

"You're living in a car?"

"It's just temporary," said Travis. "We'll be moving in a house as soon as Dad gets a job."

"Wow," she muttered. "I don't think I ever knew someone who was living in a car. Where do you take a bath?"

"We're almost there," said Melvin over his shoulder.

"Why didn't we walk?" asked Travis. "The carnival was just around the corner from where I live."

"I wanted to take my new car for a spin," said Melvin turning down a neighborhood street. "Besides, I thought we might go for a ride after dark and find someplace to park, if you know what I mean."

Travis sat back. He glanced at Sara. She was blushing and covering a smile with her hand. "Why would you want to park someplace?" he asked. Sara looked away. Travis looked into the rearview mirror and saw Melvin wink at him. "I don't get it."

Melvin brought the car to a stop. "You don't have a clue, do you?" he asked getting out of the car. The others snickered.

"About what?" asked Travis getting out of the car. The three laughed aloud as the bewildered Travis fell in step. "I have a feeling this has something to do with dating, and everyone knows what you're talking about but me."

They turned the corner and stopped just in front of a steel structure standing in the middle of Main Street. "Look at the size of that Ferris wheel!" exclaimed Melvin. "I think it's bigger than last year's." No one said anything. It was as if the entire downtown had disappeared, and these giant structures from another world had dropped down from the sky. "We'll see you two back on this spot in two hours. Okay?"

Travis nodded his head and began to walk. He watched Melvin and Linda Sue disappear into the crowd. "Can I ask you a question?" asked Travis turning to his date.

"Sure."

"How well do you know Melvin?"

"I've known him all my life. Why?"

"I don't know," said Travis looking away. "He's a good friend, but there's something about him I can't figure out."

"He's a Steelman," she blurted.

"What's that suppose to mean?"

Sara paused. "Nothing," she said.

"What do you mean by nothing? Why does everyone become so mysterious when they talk about the Steelmans?"

"It's because of Harlan. Harlan is the town bully. He gets whatever he wants, and everyone knows not to get in his way."

Travis stopped in front of a large circular structure. It slowly began to spin quickly gathering speed. Travis grimaced. "What about Melvin?" he asked turning to his date. "Melvin doesn't seem so bad."

"Melvin's dad is Harlan's brother, but that's where the similarities end. Forest became a lawyer. In fact, he's considered a very good one. How those two came from the same seed is beyond understanding."

Travis turned to the ride that was now spinning at full speed. The passengers were screaming as the seats spun in a blur.

"What about the old man?" he asked. "How did he become so rich?"

"Nolan Steelman was the biggest farmer in these parts. He was a tough and hard man but was fair and honest. Unfortunately, he's too old to run the farm anymore, so Harlan is in charge now, and Harlan is too busy with the women in town."

"My mother is going to be working for the old man," said Travis.

"Yeah, I know," she said looking away.

"How did you know?"

"It's a small town. Everyone knows everyone's business."

Travis paused. "What's the matter? Is there something wrong with my mother working out there?"

"You don't know, do you?" she asked turning in his direction.

"Don't know what?"

Sara paused. She glanced at the ground and back to Travis. "Everyone in town knows it, so I suppose you should know it too."

"Know what?" shouted Travis.

"Years ago when your mother was a kid, she dated Harlan," said Sara stopping in the middle of the street. "The story goes that they were quite an item. Some say they were even planning to get married. Then your dad came along and pretty much swept your mother off her feet. She left Harlan and married your father. Happy ending to a romantic story? Not hardly. Harlan is still carrying a torch for your mother.

Not likely he's forgotten what your daddy took away from him either."

Sara paused as she studied Travis. His face showed concern as he stared at the ground. "I'm sorry to be the one to tell you this," she said softly. "I really am, but when you mentioned that your mother was going to work for the Steelmans, I just thought you should know." Travis said nothing. He didn't move. "Travis, are you okay?"

"Yeah," he said looking up. "Yeah, I'm fine." The ride just in front of them had stopped, and people were falling in line to get on. "Come on," he said taking her by the arm. "Let's take this thing for a spin."

Sara's face went blank. "I don't think so," she said following behind.

"Come on. It will be fun," he said pulling her along.

"These things make me puke."

"You'll be fine," he said stepping into the last empty car. They both snapped the safety belt in place and grabbed the steel bar in front of them. Travis glanced up as the car began to move. A thin chain connected the car to one of many arms protruding from the center of the ride. "Jesus," he muttered as he turned to Sara. "Whose idea was this anyway?"

The cars started spinning gathering speed with each lap. Within moments, they were spinning sideways like a giant fan. Travis struggled to turn his head. Sara's face was frozen with fright. He felt his stomach turn as the cars spun even faster. He wondered how anybody could find pleasure in such an experience.

After what seemed like an eternity, the cars began to slow. As they did, they fell from the sky until they were sitting upright spinning slowly in a circle. "And they call that fun," said Travis staring at the spinning ground until it finally came to a stop. "Let's get off this thing," he said unbuckling the seatbelt.

"I think I'm going to be sick," she muttered as she bolted towards a trashcan. Travis politely turned away as she retched uncontrollably. He glanced in her direction to see her wiping her mouth with a tissue.

"Wanna sit down?" he asked.

"As long as the seat doesn't move," she said without looking up.

Travis led her to an empty park bench. "Sorry," he said taking a seat. "Just my luck. My first date, and she pukes. "

Sara breathed deeply and let it out slowly. "Got any gum?"

"No."

"Mints?"

"Sorry."

She held her hand to her face and exhaled. "Oh, my God!" she exclaimed wiping her mouth again. "My breath is so bad!"

Travis handed her his handkerchief. "I'm really sorry about this," he said. "I guess I haven't made much of an impression on you, have I?"

"Oh, you've made an impression, alright," she said wiping her face.

Travis turned away. He could see that she was upset. He cursed himself for taking her on that ride. Not even an hour into his first date and she's thrown up her dinner and thinks he's a jerk.

"Is there anything I can do?" he asked.

She dropped his handkerchief on the bench between them. She turned and stared at him with a strange look on her face. "You've done enough," she said with a smile.

"You're not mad at me anymore?" he asked with a puzzled look.

"I wasn't mad at you in the first place," she said. "After all, I didn't have to go on that ride."

"I promise that if we go on any more rides, it will be your idea," he said. Silence fell on the couple as they watched the people walk by.

"How late will your parents allow you to stay out?" he asked.

"I can stay out until eleven," she replied. "It's just my mother, you know. I live with just my mother."

"Are your folks divorced?"

"No, my dad is dead," she said softly.

"I'm sorry to hear that," said Travis. "I've done it again, haven't I?"

"What's that?"

"Said something I shouldn't have."

"Oh no, not really," she said glancing at the ground. "In fact, I'm really quite proud of what he did that cost him his life. My dad was always my hero even before this happened."

"Do you mind telling me what happened?"

"It was last winter," she said looking up. "In fact, it was New Year's Eve, and Mom and Dad were coming home from a party. Dad had been drinking. Seems strange now because Dad didn't drink. To this day, Mom cannot figure that one out. Anyway, it had been snowing all day, and the roads were slippery. Dad was driving too fast and taking chances he shouldn't have.

Do you know how Old Plank Road has that drop-off? Well, Dad took that corner a little too fast and put the car into a spin. They went through the guardrail and the car came to rest with the backend teetering over the edge of the cliff. Mom said it was perfectly balanced. If they moved even a little bit, it made the car rock."

"That's incredible," said Travis. "What happened then?"

"They sat there for several moments but could feel the car slipping. There was only time for one of them to get out. They couldn't go together because as soon as one of them would get out of the car, the loss of weight would cause it to fall backwards over the cliff. They knew that one of them was going to live and one wasn't. The real shame was they had no time to say good bye. The car was slipping and would soon fall taking both of them with it. They argued for several moments, but finally Dad forced Mom out of the car."

"My God!" muttered Travis.

"When my mother's foot touched the ground, the car began to slide," said Sara with a stone face. "She said that she nearly didn't get her other leg from the car when it plummeted over the cliff. Mom said she glanced back as the car began to fall away and for a brief moment in time she saw my dad's face staring back at her. She said my dad was smiling at her." Sara wiped her eyes with a tissue. "She said it was a smile unlike anything she had ever seen. She said it was Dad's way of saying good bye and don't worry about him, and I believe her. That would be just like Daddy to do that. That smile during that brief moment in time still haunts her to this day."

"I'm so sorry," said Travis. "I don't think I've ever heard a story quite like that one."

Sara wiped her eyes and smiled. "I'm the one who should be apologizing," she said. "What kind of story is that to tell on a first date?"

Travis turned. There was a commotion coming from the crowd. He took the young girl by the arm and got to his feet. "Let's go see what's going on," he said weaving his way through the people.

At the heart of the crowd, a space had been cleared in the middle of the street. Travis elbowed his way to the center of the disturbance. "It's Lone Wolf," he said turning to Sara, "and he's got Harlan in his face."

"So you're the famous Lone Wolf," said Harlan standing in his way. The big man stepped aside to pass, and Harlan moved as well. "I hear you can turn into a wolf. Let's see ya do it. C'mon, what's the harm? We're all here for entertainment, and what could be more entertaining than to see you do something like that."

Lone Wolf stood his ground, his face expressionless.

Harlan inched forward, nearly touching Lone Wolf. "C'mon, tough guy," he said bumping him with his chest. "Do it! Turn into a wolf!" Lone Wolf froze. He dropped his hands to his sides. "That's just what I thought," said Harlan with a loud voice. "You ain't so tough after all. All that talk about you being a wolf and all. Hell, you're just plain yella, and that's a fact.

Lone Wolf glanced down at the ground and took two steps back.

"Where are you going, Mr. Wolf Man?" shouted Harlan. "I don't remember giving you permission to walk away." Harlan pushed the big man in the chest, and he stepped back to gain his balance. "We're all still waiting to see you change into some kind of animal 'er something," he said pushing him once again. "Do it, big man!" shouted Harlan pushing Lone Wolf again. He pushed him again and again with Lone Wolf stepping backwards each time. The crowd moved with each step.

Finally, Harlan shoved Lone Wolf with both hands sending him sprawling onto the ground. The crowd grew silent. They watched intently, certain of the fight that would most certainly break out as soon as Lone Wolf could get to his feet.

Lone Wolf slowly regained his footing and stood straight, towering nearly a foot over Harlan's head. He stared down at the young man; his face was like stone. Harlan's smile disappeared. The crowd grew silent. Harlan braced himself for what he thought was sure to come. An eternity passed.

Harlan began to twitch, his legs visibly shaking. His face paled as he stepped back.

Suddenly, the big man turned and walked away, the crowd clearing a path for him to pass. All eyes watched as he disappeared down the street and then turned to Harlan. "I guess I taught him a thing or two," Harlan announced and walked away.

"Come on," said Travis grabbing Sara's arm. "Let's go catch Lone Wolf." They weaved their way through the crowd until they were at the outskirts of town, soon jogging to overtake the big man.

"Lone Wolf!" shouted Travis as he began to run. "Stop a minute! I want to talk to you!" Lone Wolf didn't miss a stride. Travis finally overtook him and grabbed him by the arm. "I just want to ask you a question," he said catching his breath.

Lone Wolf stopped in the road and turned to Travis. "What you want?" he asked.

"Why did you do that back there?" asked Travis.

"Why I do what?"

"Let Harlan push you around. You could have squashed him if had wanted to. Why did you let him get away with that?"

"He do nothing to me."

"He pushed you around," said Travis. "You can't let him do that."

"Why not?" asked Lone Wolf. "He not hurt me."

"That's not the point. He's a puke and he's a bully. That's more than enough reason to pound him."

Lone Wolf turned and started walking again. "Sorry, but he no hurt me, then I no hurt him."

"Stop!" shouted Travis grabbing the big man. Lone Wolf stopped and turned. "Make me a promise," said Travis still holding his arm. "Promise me you will kick his ass if ever does that again."

"He no hurt…"

"I know. He didn't hurt you," said Travis releasing his arm. "This isn't a question of self defense. This is a question of pride. A big guy like you shouldn't have to take crap from a weasel like Harlan. Promise me you'll pound him if he ever does that again to you."

Lone Wolf stared at the young boy for a moment. He turned to Sara. "Who that?" he asked.

"This is Sara," said Travis turning to the young woman. "Sara meet Lone Wolf."

"Nice to meet you, Lone Wolf," she said shyly.

Lone Wolf stared at her and then turned to Travis. "She your woman?"

Travis glanced at Sara. "No, not really. It's just our first date."

"You having what you call a blind date," said Lone Wolf.

"Yeah, that's right," said Travis. "It is a blind date, but how did you know?"

"She too pretty for you," said Lone Wolf with a smile.

"Oh, that's funny," said Travis shaking his head. He turned to Sara who was laughing aloud. "Now I'm getting the business from a guy who hardly speaks English."

"I go now," said Lone Wolf jumping a fence beside the road.

"Wait a second," said Travis. "I want to ask you something."

"I must go!" he shouted and disappeared into the woods.

CHAPTER 5

Monday dawned in a fiery explosion of red light stretching across a blue sky. It was nearly eight o'clock when a lone woman stepped onto the dusty porch. She peered through the screen door. It was dark inside, and there was no sign of life. She thought about turning back. Nobody would blame her if she did certainly not her husband.

She gently rapped on the screen door and listened for a response. Nothing. She waited a moment and tried again. This time she heard the sound of footsteps. It was the hard, deliberate steps of boots on a hardwood floor. It had to be Harlan. Since he seldom left the house, the old man hardly ever wore shoes. As the steps came closer, a sense of fear raced through her body, and yet, there was a certain element of excitement that she could not understand. She wanted to turn and leave and never look back, but there was a part of her that wanted to stay. Besides, what little money they had left was nearly gone, and there was very little food left.

"Well, look who's here," said Harlan from inside the dark house. "It's the new cook." Kara jumped. She stepped back from the door. "You're just in time. I'm starved."

He pushed the screen door open, and Kara caught it with one hand. She cautiously stepped inside, closing the door behind her. "Where's Nolan?" she asked still standing in the doorway.

"Nolan, is it? Everyone else in town calls him Mr. Steelman."

"He said I could call him Nolan," she said peering into the darkness. "Is he here?"

"He just got up," said Harlan starting for the kitchen. "He needs more beauty sleep than most." He folded his arms and leaned against the pantry.

Kara stepped into the doorway and snapped on the light. It was a large kitchen with an island in the center with a range. The sink and countertops were piled high with dirty dishes and cookware. A broom leaned against the island with a pile of dirt next to it. Food had dripped down the cabinets and had dried. Kara studied the room and turned to Harlan.

"Has that lived-in look, doesn't it?" he asked.

"I can't believe anyone would live like this," she muttered as she ran water into the sink.

Harlan slowly walked cross the kitchen and leaned against the island just behind Kara. "Sure have needed a woman's touch around here," he said as he studied her backside. He moved next to Kara and leaned against the sink. "So, here we are again, just like the old days."

Kara poured soap into the sink and reached for a dishcloth. "'Cept for one thing," she said turning off the water. "I'm married this time."

"Yeah, that's right," said Harlan stepping back. He glanced over her shoulder at the front of her dress. The top button was unfastened, and he could see the cleavage of her ample breasts. "So, what does John think about all this? Must be hard for a man like him to have his wife working for her former lover." He returned to the sink. This time his head was nearly touching hers. "Of course, maybe it doesn't bother him. After all, we're talking about a guy who makes his beautiful wife live in a car. How high could his standards be?"

Kara finished washing a dish and rinsed it under the hot water. "John does the best he can," she said stacking the dish on a clean towel. "I have to say he treats me right."

"Treats you right?" Harlan shouted. "You call living in a car an example of treating you right? Honey, a woman like you should be dressed in the finest clothes, and you should be eating in the best restaurants. You certainly shouldn't be washing dishes and cooking for others."

"Oh, I don't know," she said grabbing another dish. "I really don't mind. Besides, washing dishes and cooking is all I really know. Never did finish school. Hell, this is the first real job I ever had."

"And you're working for the guy who used to take you to bed," said Harlan with a smile.

Kara blushed.

"I still can't believe John is letting you do this. Did you tell him where you're working?"

"Sure. I told him."

"It just don't make sense. If you were mine, I'd never let you out of my sight."

Kara dropped more dishes into the soapy water. She turned to Harlan and smiled. "He trusts me," she said softly.

"Well, he's a damn fool," said Harlan turning away. "You're way too much of a woman to trust."

Kara frowned. "Well, that ain't a very nice thing to say."

"Honey, that's the highest compliment I can give you," he said with a smile. "There's plenty of men in this world who would do just about anything to spend a little time with you, if you know what I mean?"

Harlan leaned forward on the counter and stared at Kara. She wore a flowered-dress, the kind that women wear for everyday. It had narrow straps and a scoop neck with buttons that ran down the front. Harlan studied her breasts as she worked. They sagged from the weight and swayed as she moved from side-to-side. The buttons on her dress strained, and Harlan shifted slightly to catch a glimpse of the soft white flesh. A bead of sweat trickled down the side of his face. He could feel the blood pounding through his veins.

"You know it's not too late," he said still staring at the small opening in her dress.

Kara glanced at Harlan and smiled. "Not too late for what?" she asked coyly.

"It's not too late for us," said Harlan. "You and I were great together, and you know it."

"Harlan Steelman, I'm a married woman! You shouldn't talk to me like that!"

"Come on, Kara," said Harlan. "You know it's true. We'd be perfect together." He lightly ran his fingertips down her arm.

Kara flinched. "Don't do that," she said.

"I'll buy you diamonds and clothes," he said still stroking her arm. "Hell, I'll even buy you your own car."

Kara paused. "My very own car?" she asked looking up.

"Any car you want," said Harlan. He grabbed her by the shoulders and turned her around. "You know it's the right thing to do, Kara. Time was when we were meant for each other. Nothing has changed. You and me were meant to be together, and it can still happen."

Kara held her soapy hands in the air. "I don't know," she muttered dreamily.

Harlan moved closer backing her against the sink. "You know it's right, Karas," he said inching closer until his body was touching hers. He wrapped his arms around her and straddled her legs with his. He could feel his crotch pressing against her leg. "I've never stopped wanting you," he said slowly moving his lips towards hers.

"I don't know about this," she muttered softly.

Harlan lightly touched his lips on the soft skin of her neck. He then moved to the soft, supple area behind her ear and began to lightly run his tongue over the sensitive area.

Kara moaned. "God, it's been so long," she muttered with a breathy voice.

"Much too long," he said kissing her neck again.

She was breathing heavily now nearly out of breath. She turned to face him; her parted lips only inches from his. "This isn't right," she whispered.

"Yes, it is right, and you know it is," he said softly as he pressed his lips against hers. Kara wrapped her arms around him, her wet hands soaking his shirt. They kissed passionately, their bodies writhing against each other. Harlan lightly cupped one of her breasts with his hand. He could feel the hard nipple as her body heaved with passion. He thrust one of his legs between hers pushing her dress up to her waist and softly rubbed his hard crotch against her soft thigh.

"Oh, God," she sighed as she began to move her hips with his.

Harlan fumbled with the buttons on the front of her dress. His hands shook as he unfastened the top two buttons. He pulled the top of the dress back and reached inside. He cupped his hand around the soft underside of her huge breast and lightly freed it from her clothes. Harlan bent over and gently kissed her erect nipple.

Kara's whole body heaved as she gasped for air. "Oh, my dear God," she said between gulps of air.

Suddenly, she stiffened, and her eyes opened wide. "I can't do this!" she shouted with a sober voice. "It just ain't right!"

Harlan pulled back his head and stared in shock. "What?" he asked with a raspy voice.

Kara pushed him back and covered her breast with her hand. "I'm married, and I have a son," she said pulling down her dress. "What we're doing here just ain't right."

"I don't care if it's right or not!" shouted Harlan. "It's going to happen all the same!" He pressed his lips against hers. She turned away and pushed him back. A look of anger crossed his face as he reached for her dress and violently pulled on it. Buttons popped and fell onto the floor as the dress opened wide. Harlan stepped back and smiled as he stared at her soft white skin.

"Please don't do this!" she shouted as she pushed him once again.

Harlan pinned her to the wall with one arm and began to unfasten his belt with the other. "This thing is going to happen whether you like it or not."

Kara turned her head and found his arm that had her pinned to the wall. She sunk her teeth into his flesh. He screamed and pulled away. "Goddamn you!" he shouted and glanced at his hand. Two small dots of blood surfaced. "You're going to pay for that!" he shouted and doubled his hand into a fist.

Before he could pull his arm back to strike, a ball bat crashed against his back. The force of the blow sent him sprawling onto the floor.

Kara watched in horror as Harlan fell to the floor. She looked up to a man standing in front of her still holding the bat with both hands. "Mr. Steelman!" she shouted as she stared at the man.

"Are you alright?" he asked.

She glanced at the man on the floor and then at the man in front of her. "I guess so," she finally managed to say.

Harlan groaned as he slowly got on his knees.

Kara froze as she stared at the old man still holding the bat. She glanced down at her own nudity and in a fit of embarrassment quickly covered herself with her dress. "I have to go," she said as she bowed her head in humility. She rushed past the old man and out the front door.

◆◆◆

It was already late morning when the young couple picked their way through the weeds and found themselves at the river's edge. The riverbank was slippery and uneven, so Travis gave his hand to Sara for support. They followed the winding trail until they came to a small clearing that was covered with sand and small stones and nearly on the same level as the water.

"This is my most favorite spot in the world," said Travis sitting on a fallen tree. "My dad used to come here when he was a young boy."

Sara examined the area and smiled. "It is beautiful and so peaceful," she said turning to Travis. "You don't talk much about your father. Do you get along with him?"

"Sure, we get along," said Travis as he picked at loose bark on the tree. "Why do you ask?"

"Oh, I don't know. Just call it intuition. Somehow I got the feeling that you two weren't close," she said. "I'd have to say my dad was my hero. No question about it. There was and never will be a man greater than my dad." She paused and stared across the gently flowing river. "God, I miss him."

Travis glanced at his friend and back to a piece of loose bark. "I miss my hero too," he muttered.

Sara turned in his direction. "Who was that?" she asked. "Who was your hero?"

"Oh, you don't want to know," he said. "It's really no big deal."

"Yes, it is," she said. "If he's your hero, he must be somebody important."

"That's just it," said Travis looking across the river. "He wasn't anybody important. He was never rich or owned anything great. In fact, I don't think he even owned the house he was living in when he died. He was my grandfather, and to me he was and always will be my hero."

Sara took his hand. "He must have been quite a man," she said. "What was he like?"

"He was the kind of man who had one of those forever smiles. You know the kind. When you look at them, if they aren't smiling, their eyes are."

"Did you spend much time with him?"

Travis took her hand and squeezed it tightly with both of his hands. "Not enough," he said softly. "We used to walk down the railroad tracks together. On a warm Sunday afternoon, there wasn't much to do, so we would take off down the tracks. God, I used to love those walks. It was just he and I. We'd talk a mile a minute and didn't have a care in the world. I'll bet we would walk ten miles sometimes. Funny, it didn't seem that far.

I remember this one Sunday in early spring. We were walking the tracks and had gone about a mile out of town when we came across a young deer lying dead near the tracks. We stopped and knelt down beside the body. It was a doe, and her body was still warm. The last train that had gone through only minutes before must have killed her. Obviously, she had tried to get across the tracks ahead of the oncoming train and had lost the race.

We knelt there by the dead animal in silence for several minutes. I was busy trying to recreate in my mind what had happened. Why did this beautiful animal take such a risk? What was so important that she would risk and ultimately give her life in such a dangerous act?

I, then, began to realize what we had found. This was fresh meat. Enough meat to last for a long time. My mind began to whirl. Who could we get to process it? How would I get it back to town in time? After all, it was a warm day. That meat wouldn't stay fresh for long.

I was proudly standing over the fallen animal as if I had slain it myself when I heard my grandfather quietly sobbing. I glanced down at him and noticed he was looking not at the fallen deer, but across a meadow that was near the railroad tracks. I couldn't imagine what he could possibly be looking at until I looked across the field myself. There at the edge of a small grove of trees was a small spotted fawn. He had wandered out of the safety of the woods and into the open field. His head was held high as he searched in all directions. After a few moments, the young animal dropped its head and bolted back into the woods. You know, I'd give anything if I could go back in time. If I could, I would go back to that moment and do it all over again."

"I don't understand, Travis," said Sara. "What would you do differently?"

"It's simple," he said. "I would have cried with him. Out there on that warm Spring day, I saw meat on the table and he saw life at a most tender moment. God forgive me for letting that moment slip away."

Sara stared across the river and then turned to Travis. "It sounds as if your grandfather was quite a man," she said softly.

"Yes, he was," said Travis. He paused for a moment, and then as if to change the tempo, he said, "So, how do you like my little world here in the woods? You know my dad used to swim in this river when he was a kid."

"Have you ever gone swimming in this river?" she asked.

"All the time," he replied.

"I have an idea," she said with a smile. "Let's you and I go."

"Go where?"

"Go swimming."

Travis glanced across the river and back at the young woman in front of him. "We don't have swimsuits," he said quietly.

"We don't need them," she said with a smile. "We'll go skinny-dippin'."

Travis could feel his face flush. "We can't do that," he said.

"Why not? It'll be fun."

"I can't…"

"You can't what?"

Travis stared at the ground. "I can't undress in front of you."

"You're not going to," she said playfully slapping him on the arm. "You're going down river behind those bushes. I'll undress right here, and I'll meet you in the water. How deep is it anyway?"

"Well, out there in the middle of the river, it gets up to here," he said holding his hand at his chest. "On you, it should cover your…" He paused. "It should be high enough."

Sara smiled. "It should be high enough for what?"

Travis looked away. "You know," he muttered.

Sara laughed. "Yes, I know," she said and began to unbutton her blouse. "Now, unless you plan to only talk about it, I suggest you go get undressed." Travis stared as she quickly unfastened the buttons. "Well!" she shouted.

Travis disappeared around the bend in the river. He hid behind a forsythia bush and began to remove his socks and shoes. He then pulled off his shirt and hung it on a low-lying branch as he had done so many times before. He unfastened his belt and pulled his zipper down halfway and stopped. He cautiously leaned forward and peeked around the bush. He could not see Sara, but more importantly she could not see him. He removed his pants and hung them on the branch beside his shirt.

Travis stared down at his faded under shorts. If he takes them off, she might regard him as too bold, a loose character with no morals. If he leaves them on, he's old-fashioned, a prude with sexual hang-ups. He hooked his thumbs in the waistband and stared in her direction. With a quick thrust, he pulled his shorts halfway down his legs his thumbs still holding on. He paused and glanced at the slow-moving water. "Bet it's cold," he muttered and pulled up his shorts.

Travis walked to the edge of the water. He turned as he heard water splashing and screams of laughter. It was Sara. Panic struck him as he imagined her swimming down river enough to see him standing at the water's edge in his underwear. The young man shuffled his feet as fast as he could wading into the river until the water was near his waist and then dove head first.

"Christ!" he shouted as his head broke the surface. "That water is cold!"

Sara laughed. She was less than fifty feet away with water up to her neck. "The water feels good," she said bouncing up and down. "It feels a lot better than it looks."

Travis leaned into the water and began to swim. "Never really cared for that shade of green," he said stopping in front of her. "I try not to think of what might be floating by."

"What do you mean?" she asked.

Travis pointed upstream. "The town's sewage dumps out about a mile that way," he said.

"Dumps where?"

"Here."

"Where's here?"

"The river," said Travis. "It dumps right into the river."

Sara glanced up the river. "That's disgusting!" she shouted. "Tell me you're kidding!"

Travis smiled. "I'm kidding," he said.

Sara paused and then smiled. "You're rotten!" she said as she splashed water in his face.

"Had ya goin', didn't I?" he asked. "Wouldn't doubt that it's true just the same. It's just something I prefer not to know the truth about."

Sara did not reply. She stared at the young man with a smile that puzzled Travis. "So, did you do it?" she asked.

"Did I do what?"

"No, I don't know what."

"Did you take everything off?"

"What do you mean?"

"You know exactly what I mean. Are you completely naked?"

Travis looked away. "Well, not exactly."

"You're wearing your underwear, aren't you?" Before he could reply, she reached into the pale green water and snapped the elastic on his underwear. "I don't believe it! I thought we agreed to take everything off."

"I didn't want you to think of me as too forward."

"Don't think there's much fear of that," she said. She paused and smiled. "I'm not wearing anything," she said. "Do you want to see?"

"No, I don't want to see," he said quickly. "I mean I believe you."

"Give me your hand," she announced.

"What for?"

"Just give it to me," she said taking his hand in hers. She guided his outstretched fingers down her side and over her hip. "See, I told you. I'm not wearing a thing."

Her soft, tender skin felt good to the touch. Travis could feel the blood pounding through his veins as he quickly withdrew his hand. "I shouldn't be doing that."

"Doing what?"

"Touching you like that. It ain't right."

"Why? You didn't touch anything bad."

"It still ain't right."

The young woman stared at Travis. "You've never dated any girl before me, have you?"

"Not really," he replied looking away.

Sara paused. "Let me ask you something. Have you ever kissed a girl?"

"Kiss my aunts all the time."

"I'm talking about a girl not a relative. Have you ever kissed a girl?"

"Not really."

"Do you want to?" she asked with a smile.

"When?"

"Right now. Would you like to kiss me right now?"

"I suppose so," he said shyly.

"Suppose so!" she shouted. "Doesn't say much for me! I was hoping for something a little more positive than that!"

"I'm sorry," he said. "It's just that I've never done anything like this."

"Come here," she said reaching out with both hands. "Put your arms around me."

Travis cautiously encircled her with his arms lightly resting them on her lower back. Sara said nothing. A slight smile appeared as she stared into the young man's eyes. Travis could feel his body quiver with excitement as he slowly bent over. He lightly pressed his lips to hers for only a moment and quickly retreated. He stared down at the young woman. The smile was gone, her lips slightly parted. This time she pulled him to her and kissed him hard her tongue probing his parted lips. She pulled his body close to hers. He could feel the valley between her legs against him, and her hard nipples lightly brushing his chest.

Travis grabbed her passionately and pulled her close. He could feel the heat of passion as her tongue thrust in and out of his mouth. His hands followed the contour of her back. They glided over her hips and came to rest on her soft, almond-shaped buttock. He freed one hand and started slowly up her side and around to her stomach. His hand was shaking as he brought it to her lower chest and stopped.

Suddenly, they both jumped at the sound of a voice. "Hey, Travis! Where the hell are you?" They turned to see Melvin sliding down the bank of the river. He stopped at the river's edge and stared at the couple. "I hate to interrupt whatever you two were doing, but I have something important to tell you."

"What is it?" asked Travis turning in his direction.

"I probably shouldn't be telling you this, but seeing how you're my friend I feel you should know," said Melvin.

"I should know what?"

Melvin took a long breath. "I heard Grandpa telling Dad. Uncle Harlan kinda attacked your mother."

"He what?" shouted Travis.

"I guess he tried to rape her. Grandpa broke it up before anything happened."

"Where's Mom?"

"She went home. I guess she's okay. Just a little upset."

"Where's your uncle?" asked Travis his jaw tensed.

"Probably on his third beer down at Moonies."

With giant strides, Travis waded ashore. "Walk Sara home for me, will ya, Melvin?" he asked. "I need to go kick your uncle's ass."

"You be careful around him, Travis," he said. "You don't want to mess with Harlan Steelman."

Travis pulled on his pants and shirt and bent over to slip on his shoes. "I really don't care," he snapped.

Melvin walked over and placed a hand on his shoulder. "I'm just telling you to just watch yourself. He's mean, and he fights dirty."

"And I'm telling you I really don't care!" Travis shouted. He took one step and turned. "What if it was your mother?"

◆◆◆

It was early afternoon when Abe, the bartender, turned the key on the front door. Moonies was officially open for business. Harlan Steelman leaned back and drained the last drop of beer from the bottle and slammed it on the bar. "Set me up another one," he said to the man behind the bar.

"You're going to fry your liver if you don't ease up on that stuff," said the man sitting next to him.

Harlan turned in his seat. "What are you talking about? Not all those empty bottles are mine, you know."

Howard Bailey smiled. "It's different with me," he said. "An old alcoholic ain't nearly as disgusting as a young one."

Harlan chuckled aloud. "Got to die some how," he said. "I guess alcoholism is as good a way as any."

Howard gulped his beer. "Always figured you'd go at the hands of a jealous husband."

"What are you talking about?" asked Harlan. "I only have two rules that I live by. Don't clip your fingernails over the dinner table and don't mess around with another man's wife."

"You're so full of shit," said Howard. "There isn't a woman in town you haven't screwed. I'm surprised someone hasn't cut off your dick by now."

Suddenly, the front door exploded open, and Travis stood in the open doorway. "Harlan Steelman!" he shouted.

The two men spun around on their stools. Harlan gulped his beer. "Who's asking?"

"I'm the guy who's gonna kick your ass!" he shouted and with doubled fists started across the floor.

Harlan scrambled to his feet. "Now hold on there, boy," he said holding out one hand. "I ain't done nothing to you."

Travis swung a fist at the man. He dodged it and pushed Travis to the floor. "Now, I don't know who you are, boy, but you're going to get hurt," said Harlan.

Travis scrambled to his feet and charged at the man again. Harlan grabbed him by the shirt and threw him to the floor. He stepped over to the bar and gulped from his beer bottle. "Now, why don't you just get out of here, son," said Harlan. "I'm getting real tired of this."

Travis got to his feet. He crouched in a fighting stance his face flush with anger. He reached for an empty beer bottle and grabbed it by the neck. "I'm going to kill you," he said raising the bottle over his head.

"Okay, boy," said Harlan raising his fists. "I warned you."

Travis swung the empty bottle, and Harlan blocked it with his arm. With his doubled fist, he jabbed Travis in the stomach dropping him to the floor. He gasped violently for air and got to his knees. With one giant stride, Harlan charged the young man and struck him in the head with his fist. The blow sent Travis reeling backwards with blood splattering the wall. He rolled over and slowly got to his knees his head dripping blood to the floor.

Harlan grabbed his hair and pulled back his head. "Had enough?" he asked. Travis said nothing. Harlan pulled back his fist, but before he could strike, he heard the front door open. He turned and saw a man standing in the open doorway.

"Maybe, it's time you picked on someone more your size," said John Watson letting the door close behind him.

Harlan turned and smiled. "I've been waiting for this for a long time," he said walking slowly across the room. The two men crouched into a fighting posture and circled each other their fists raised for combat. "I'm going to hurt you, John Watson."

John stopped and braced his back foot. "Stop talking about it and do something," he taunted.

Harlan took two steps and pulled back his right fist.

"What's going on here?" boomed a voice from the doorway. The two men paused and turned. A short, fat man in a uniform stood in the open doorway with one hand holding the door. "Looks to me like there's a problem here," he said slowly walking across the floor.

"Not at all, Sheriff," said Harlan dropping his hands to his sides. "We're just foolin' around. That's all."

Sheriff Miller turned to John who had taken a cue from Harlan and had relaxed as well. "You're John Watson, aren't you?" he asked studying the man.

"That's me," he replied.

"I've heard about you," said the Sheriff stopping in front of John. "You're the one living in the car, ain't 'cha?"

"Guilty as charged," John replied with a smile.

The Sheriff turned and winked at Harlan. "Guilty is probably a good choice of words," he said. "I could run you in for vagrancy. Can't live in a car in this town. Besides, I'm not so sure I want the likes of you in this town." He turned to Harlan and back. "Looks to me like you're in here botherin' these people. Any truth to that, Harlan?"

"We were just sittin' here having a beer when John here walked in and wanted to fight," said Harlan. "I ain't quite sure what his problem is. All I know is that I don't want no trouble with anybody."

The Sheriff turned to John. "Alright, Mr. Watson, you heard the man. What seems to be the trouble?"

John turned to Harlan and then back to the Sheriff. "Not that it will do any good to report it, but this man tried to rape my wife," he said through tight lips. He pointed at Harlan. "And either the law is going to do something about it or I will."

"Well, Harlan," said the Sheriff. "This man has made a pretty serious accusation about you. What do you have to say for yourself?"

Harlan smiled. "Hell, Sheriff," he said leaning against the bar. "You know me. I'm a goddamn alcoholic. I've been here since early this morning. I haven't even seen his wife today." He turned to John. "Not that I wouldn't like to."

John clenched his fists. His jaw tightened. "You stay the hell away from her!" he shouted. He pointed his finger at Harlan. "You touch my wife again, and I'll kill you!"

"Hey, boy," said the Sheriff holding up one hand as if he were stopping traffic. "That's enough of that kind of talk. Hell, I could run you in for that alone."

"Well, I can see how things are in this town," said John walking to the front door. He opened it and looked back over his shoulder. "A man tries to rape my wife, and you want to arrest me. Seems real clear to me what's going on here." He paused waiting for a reaction. Both men smirked and said nothing. John turned and let the door close behind him.

CHAPTER 6

It was early evening when a red pick up turned down the dusty alley. John and Kara were sitting on broken kitchen chairs when the vehicle stopped just in front of them. An older man climbed out and came around the side of the truck hobbling as he walked. "I guess I'm getting too old to even walk any more," he said stopping in front of the two people. He leaned against the hood of the car. "Can't even remember the last time I left the house." He paused and waited for a response. "Gonna be a pretty sunset," he said looking up at the sky. "Them clouds over there, the way they seem to stack up one layer on the other. They'll shine when that sun turns them red. Prettiest damn thing in the world to see. Don't you agree?"

John turned in his chair. "Got no quarrel with you, Mr. Steelman," said John without getting up. "Just not in the mood to deal with a Steelman right now."

"Can't say as I blame you," he said removing his hat with one hand and wiping the inside with his other. "Call me Nolan. Mr. Steelman sounds so formal. Hell, we've known each other much too long to be talking that way. Seems like only yesterday you were a young pup running barefoot through town."

Nolan paused for a reaction. John smiled politely but said nothing.

Nolan turned to Kara. "I know it wasn't a very good day for you, Kara, and for that I'm very sorry," he said as he set his hat on the hood of the car. "That boy of mine ain't got the brains he was born with, and this ain't the first time I've had to apologize for him. All the same, I still want you to work for me."

"Ain't no way in the world!" shouted John turning in his direction. "After what we've been through with that son of yours, there's no way I would let my wife be around him again."

Nolan slowly walked over to a tree stump and sat down. He reached into his shirt pocket and pulled out a cigarette. "John, I understand what you're saying," said Nolan as he stuck a lighted match to his cigarette. "I probably would be of the same mind if it were me. All I'm asking is to give me another chance. I kicked Harlan out of the house. In fact, he's already moved into the barn. Seems only fitting that the likes of him live in a barn with the rest of the animals. Trust me on this, John. I promise nothing will happen to Kara."

John paused. He turned his chair to face his visitor. "Why, Nolan?" he asked. "Why are you doing this? Most people would just let it drop. Most people would be too embarrassed to face us right now under the circumstances."

Nolan smiled. "You're good people," he said knocking the ashes from his cigarette. A solemn look spread across his face. "This town has more than its share of Harlan Steelmans. What it needs is to find more folks like you. If this town is ever going to survive, we need to somehow attract young families to our town, which brings me to the second reason I'm here. I own the old McKinley house over on Elm Street. It's been empty now for over a year. Ain't too fancy, but it's a roof over the head, no matter how much it leaks. What do you say, John? Would you like to move in there until you get on your feet?"

John smiled, his face relaxed. "That's awfully nice of you, Nolan," he said. "But I'm afraid I can't afford something like that."

"Couldn't take money from you," said Nolan inhaling his cigarette. "Just want you to have a place to live in for a while. Who knows? You might end up buying the place from me."

John paused. He smiled and turned to Kara. "What do you think?" he asked.

She turned to Nolan and back to her husband. "I think that's just about the nicest thing anybody has done for us since we came here."

John stood and faced his visitor. He thrust his hand in his direction. "Mr. Nolan, we'd be proud to move into your house," said John with a smile.

Nolan got to his feet and grabbed his hand. "If there's anything more I can do for you just let me know," he said as he handed him the keys to the house.

It was early the next morning when the old, rusted stationwagon stopped in front of a small ranch house. It was obvious from its appearance that it had been abandoned for quite some time. The windows were boarded over and the weeds were knee high. John unlocked the door and swung it open sending a whirpool of dust across the wooden floor. He turned to the light switch by the door. Years of dirt and fingerprints covered the switch and the wall.

John turned to his wife. "What do you think?" he asked.

She walked across the room and stepped into the kitchen pausing to look around. "Needs a lot of work," she said turning to John. She slowly nodded her head and smiled. "But I think we can make a home out of it."

John smiled back.

"Can I go for a walk?" asked Travis.

"Just for a short while," said his mother. "We've got lots of work to do, and we need your help."

Travis opened the front door. "I'll be back in an hour or so," he said and closed the door behind him.

It was a quiet neighborhood the streets lined on both sides with tall maKaratic elm trees. The only sounds were that of a barking dog and the low hum of a lawnmower somewhere in the distance. Travis turned the corner and started up the next street. For the most part, the lawns were neat and clean with only an occasional yard that was ill kept.

Travis was halfway up the street when he came to a stop. There lying face down on a blanket was a young blonde-haired woman wearing only the bottoms of a two-piece swimsuit. The top had been unfastened in the back, and the two straps were lying on either side of her. Travis squinted and leaned forward. She had a dark tan except for a thin band of white skin that ran across her back and plunged down to her bulging breasts.

Travis was frozen in his tracks. He looked both ways to be certain he was alone. A bead of sweat trickled down the side of his face as he turned his attention back to the woman. Glistening with sweat her soft back tapered to her almond-shaped hips, her round buttock rising maKaratically.

Travis looked up. A speeding car careened around the corner and screeched to a stop. Melvin Steelman leaned out the open window and smiled at his wide-eyed friend.

"What's the matter with you?" he asked with a puzzled look.

Travis said nothing. He pointed at the woman lying on the ground.

Melvin looked up. "Holy Moly," he said with a hushed voice. His mouth dropped open. Travis turned and smiled.

"Why hasn't she looked up?" asked Melvin. "She has to have heard us."

"She has a portable radio right beside her," replied Travis.

Melvin pointed at the woman and said, "Keep your eyes on her." Travis gave him a puzzled look. Still pointing Melvin extended his arm out the window."Turn your head around and watch!" he exclaimed with a hushed shout. Travis turned to the woman still lying face down.

With both hands Melvin slammed the horn of his car. The young woman raised up her breasts swaying beneath her.

"Wow," muttered Travis his mouth gaping open.

The woman strained to see into the car. "Is that you, Melvin Steelman?" she asked her breasts still exposed.

Melvin cleared his throat. "Yeah, it's me," he said shyly.

She covered her breasts with a towel and sat up on the blanket. "Pretty neat trick, Melvin," she said with a smile. "Has it ever worked before, or am I the only sucker?"

He turned down the radio on his car. "Couple times," he said.

She picked up the blanket and a bottle of suntan lotion and got to her feet. "Would you and your friend like to come inside for something cold to drink?" she asked with a breathy voice.

Melvin tapped the side of his car. He glanced at Travis to see if he was interested but found himself staring at the face of a young man still in shock. "Yeah, sure," he said turning back to the woman. She turned and walked slowly to the backdoor of her house.

Melvin got out of his car and walked over to his friend. "Come on, Travis, snap out of it. This woman is hot," he said grabbing his arm. "I think she wants us to screw her. My God, can you believe it? That beautiful woman wants us to do it to her!"

Travis glanced at the house. "Yeah, how 'bout that?"

"What do you think she wants us to do? Do you think she wants us to double-team her or one at a time? Huh? What do you think?"

Travis slowly turned back to his friend. "I don't know," he muttered.

Melvin frowned. "Hey, what's the matter with you?" he asked. "You're not turning chicken on me, are you?"

Travis paused. He quickly glanced at the house. "I just don't think we should go in there."

Melvin grabbed Travis with both hands. "Now, Travis, I want you to look at me," he said his face set in a deep frown. "I need a good reason from you of why we shouldn't go in there. My God, man, this is the chance of a lifetime."

Travis glanced at the ground. "I just can't."

"You have to do better than that."

Travis turned to the house. "I have a problem," he said quietly.

"Good God, Travis, what is it?"

"I…I'm…"

"You're still a virgin, aren't you?"

"Well, kinda."

"Guess what? There's no such thing as kinda a virgin," said Melvin with a smile. "Besides, what's the problem? This is perfect. She'll break your cherry, and you don't have to look like such a loser when you do it with whats-her-face."

"I don't know," he muttered.

Melvin took Travis by the arm and started for the door. "There's no I don't know to it," he said. "This doesn't happen everyday to guys like us in Bumpkinville, USA. Now, come on." Travis balked. "I said let's go!" he shouted and pulled on his arm. The two boys walked slowly across the backyard and up the steps. Melvin grabbed the handle and cautiously opened the backdoor.

"Come on in," she announced reaching for two drinking glasses. "How's lemonade sound to you? I just made it."

The two boys stepped inside the door. "That sounds great," said Melvin his eyes searching the kitchen.

She was a tall woman with long, lean legs. Her blonde hair flowed over her shoulders softly curling at the ends. She had wrapped the towel around her chest and had folded one end inside. It was a small towel revealing cleavage at the top and hung down to her thighs.

She finished pouring the lemonade and slid the two glasses across the kitchen counter. "So, Melvin, who's your new friend and what are you doing on this side of town?"

Melvin walked slowly across the floor and took one of the glasses. He sipped from the glass as he turned to Travis. "This here's Travis, and we're just kinda goofin' around. You know, nothing much to do, so we're just hangin' out."

"Just hanging out," she said leaning against the stove. She turned to Travis. "My name is Liz."

"Nice to meet you," said Travis his voice breaking.

The smile disappeared from her lips as she stared intently at Travis. "You're kind of cute," she said as a matter of fact. Melvin turned abruptly to examine his friend for anything that might be considered cute. "You're new around here. Where did you come from?"

"Little Falls," he blurted.

Liz picked up her half empty glass of lemonade and took a sip still staring at Travis. "You're not the one who lives in the car with your parents, are you?"

"We did at one time, but we moved into a house around the block."

Liz took another sip of lemonade. "Seem awful nervous," she said softly. "What do you plan on doing?"

"Nothing," he blurted. "I or we just stopped in for some lemonade. It's really hot out and we're really thirsty, aren't we, Melvin?"

"Yeah, that's right," said Melvin turning to Liz.

"Then, why don't you come over here and get your drink?" she asked.

Travis walked slowly across the room and picked up the glass of lemonade. "Thanks," he said as he stared at the drink.

Liz smiled. "What's wrong?" she asked leaning forward. "You don't think I've put poison in there, do you?"

Travis gulped down the drink. "Just checking for seeds," he said returning the glass to the counter.

Liz turned and smiled at Melvin. "So, tell me, Melvin," she said slowly sipping her drink. "What are you really here for? I know you didn't stop in for no lemonade. Your Uncle Harlan stops in here from time to time, and he don't want no lemonade."

Melvin turned to Travis. "My friend and I were just wonderin' if maybe you could show us a good time. Of course, we ain't no virgins. Fact is, we've been with lots of girls, but that's the problem. They've all been just girls. We want to experience a real woman."

Liz refilled her drink and leaned on the counter next to Melvin. "You know I don't do this kind of thing for nothing," she said her voice suddenly taking on a serious tone.

"How much will this cost us?" asked Melvin removing his billfold from his back pocket.

"How much do you have?"

He searched thorough his wallet counting the bills. "I have ten dollars."

Liz stopped. She studied the two young boys in her kitchen. Travis was wringing his hands as sweat ran down the side of his face. Melvin smiled. It was the smile of a hunter as he stands over his kill.

"I'll tell you what," she said. "Ten bucks normally wouldn't even be a down payment, but today I'm feeling generous. Now, tell me. What protection do you have?"

Melvin glanced at Travis. His blank stare told him everything he needed to know. "We don't need any protection," said Melvin. "He watches my back, and I cover his."

Liz laughed aloud. "No, you sillies!" she shouted. "I'm talking about Trojans." The two boys glanced at one another.

"You know… rubbers. You do know what rubbers are, don't you?"

"Oh, yes," said Melvin with a voice of confidence. He began to dig in his wallet. "I believe I have my ticket to paradise," he announced holding up a small square package between two fingers."

Liz turned to Travis. "What about you?"

"I don't have anything like that," said Travis.

"I don't believe it," said Melvin. "Every guy carries one. You can't take a chance of not having one when something likes this happens."

"I don't even know what they are."

Melvin slowly shook his head. "You dumb ass! You slide it over your dick."

"Really? What does it look like?"

Melvin glanced at Liz and then turned to Travis. "It's like one finger from a plastic glove only bigger."

"Where do you get them?"

"I get mine from my wallet. You will get yours down at Clark's Drug Store."

Travis turned to Liz. He hoped to find her frowning in protest of what Melvin was saying. Unfortunately, she was nodding her head in agreement. "They sell such things in a drug store?" he asked in disbelief.

"Yeah," said Melvin, "and good luck if old man Clark is there. He likes to humiliate young boys who come in there to buy rubbers."

"Oh, Christ," muttered Travis. "Well, I guess I'll get going," he said and started for the door. "What are you going to do until I get back?"

Melvin glanced at Liz and started to laugh.

"Oh, yeah," said Travis and walked out the door. He bound down the steps and hit the sidewalk running. He had made it down the street and around the corner when he suddenly came to a stop. "Damn!" he shouted. He dug his hands into his pockets. "How much money do I have and how much do rubbers cost?" He pulled out two one-dollar bills and some loose change. "That should do it," he muttered and turned a corner that took him to the downtown area.

He flew down the street past the library and Laundromat and stopped in front of a small building with empty show windows. He glanced at the sign above the door that read: Clark's Drug Store. He opened the door and walked inside. It was a small drug store with a checkered tile floor and one counter that ran down the center of the sales floor. Merchandise was displayed on both sides of the counter and across all four walls. At the back of the store was another small glass counter with one cash register on top.

Travis walked over to one of the displays and picked up a tube of toothpaste. There were many women wandering around browsing at the merchandise obviously waiting for their prescriptions to be filled. Travis pretended to read the box of toothpaste as he searched the wall for anything that might be called rubbers.

He heard someone shuffling out of the backroom. It was old man Clark. He was carrying a small vial and set it down next to the register. "Mrs. Grimes," he announced and dropped the bottle into a small white bag.

Without looking up, Travis slowly moved closer to the back of the store. He stopped just short of the cash register and picked up a bottle of aspirin. Mr. Clark collected money from Mrs. Grimes and slammed the register drawer closed. Startled, Travis looked up. Mr. Clark was glaring at him. It was the kind of stare that said, "Put down that merchandise!"

Travis didn't move. His eyes were fixed on the man standing at the register. He was a middle-aged man with jet-black hair that seemed to curl and scatter in all directions. In spite of its appearance, it was said that he spent a great amount of time every morning grooming it. His face was rugged with a square jaw, and he had large bushy eyebrows that ran together in the middle.

"Can I help you?" barked the man still staring at Travis.

Travis set down the bottle he was holding and walked over to the counter. He frantically scanned the merchandise behind the register.

"Well!" demanded the man in the white smock.

Travis pulled the money from his pocket and carefully laid it on the counter top. He turned and discovered that a line had formed behind him consisting of three women, one of which he was certain lived two doors down from his new house.

"I want some rubbers," he muttered.

"What?" asked Mr. Clark.

"I want some rubbers!" he blurted.

Mr. Clark glanced at the women in line who had grown silent and were staring at the young boy at the front of the line. "What kind?" he asked leaning down and opening the glass showcase under the register.

Travis stared down through the scratched and dirty counter top. "There they are," he muttered. "I'll take the Trojans."

"What size?" asked Mr. Clark.

"What size?" Travis repeated. "What do you mean what size?"

"Small, medium, or large."

Travis turned. The two women at the end of the line were now on either side of him. "Medium," he muttered. Mr. Clark leaned down to pull a package from the case. "No, make it a large." The older man straightened and leaned on the counter with both hands his face a look of exasperation. One of the women whispered something, and the others fought back laughter. Travis leaned back and held up his head. "I still want a large," he announced.

Mr. Clark picked the small package from the showcase and slipped it into a small white paper bag. Travis felt relieved in spite of the fact that everyone in the store knew its contents. He paid for his purchase and was out the door.

Melvin was sitting on the back steps when Travis walked up still carrying his small white bag. He stared at Melvin with a puzzled look. For someone who had just made love with a woman, he didn't seem too happy.

"Your turn," said Melvin pointing at the back door with his thumb.

Travis walked slowly up the steps and opened the door. There was no one in the kitchen. He closed the door behind him. "Liz," he called.

"In here," was the muffled reply. "I'm in the bedroom."

Travis walked slowly down the hallway and turned into an open doorway. Liz was in bed with only a sheet covering her. The towel she was wearing was lying on the floor next to the bed.

"Did you get it?" she asked leaning over on one elbow.

"Did I get what?"

"You know. Did you get a rubber?"

"Yeah, I got one," he said holding it up with two fingers.

"Great, now put it on and get in bed with me," she said leaning back against the headboard.

Travis stared at the woman and then at the small package in his hand. He sat on the edge of the bed with his back to her and started to open the package. It was heavy plastic, and Travis struggled to get it open. He twisted and pulled on it with both hands. He tried tearing a corner with his teeth but still nothing.

"What's the matter?" she asked.

"I can't get it open."

"Let me try," she said. Travis leaned over and handed it to her. She struggled with the package twisting and pulling with no success. She reached over to the table beside the bed and picked up a pair of scissors. With the package at an angle, she made one cut lopping off a corner. She opened the torn package and unrolled its contents.

"Oh, my God!" Travis exclaimed. "You cut the rubber. It's full of holes."

"I did it on purpose," she said sitting up in bed.

"Why?"

"You've got an excuse to give your friend for not having sex with me."

"Yeah, but I wanted to do it."

"No, you didn't," she said. "You don't want your first time to be with a woman like me. Sex is a beautiful experience to be shared with someone you love. Don't cheapen it by screwing someone. Do me a favor and wait until your wedding night and make love to a woman you really care about. Would you do that for me?"

Travis paused as he stared at the woman. "I suppose so," he muttered. Surprisingly, he felt a certain relief. "I guess I'll go now," he said getting to his feet.

"Here, take this," said Liz tossing the torn prophylactic across the bed. "No guy in the world would blame you for not going through with it with something like this."

Travis smiled as he grabbed it from the bed. "Thanks...I think," he said as he opened the door and closed it behind him.

"Well, how was it?" asked Melvin getting to his feet.

"How was what?"

"You know. How was your first time?"

"Didn't happen," said Travis turning on to the sidewalk.

"Didn't happen!" shouted Melvin nearly running to keep up. "Why? What did happen?"

Travis held up the prophylactic with holes. "It got cut with the scissors."

"God, what a dumb ass!" Melvin shouted. "How could you let something like that happen? You're still a virgin through your own fault."

"So, what happened to you?" asked Travis. "Did you get laid?"

Melvin stopped at the side of his car. "Here, get in. We'll go for a ride," he said sliding into the driver's seat.

Travis stopped at the side of the car. He stared at his friend with a puzzled look. "Maybe, you didn't hear the question."

"I heard the question. Now, get in the car."

Travis leaned over. "Did you get laid or not?"

Melvin reached in his pocket and pulled out a prophylactic. It had been unrolled and was full of holes. "Was in my wallet too long," he said. "Now, will you get in the car?"

Travis began to laugh as he walked around the front of the car. "We're both losers," he said sliding across the seat. "We had a chance with a beautiful woman, and we blew it!"

Melvin pulled slowly away from the curb. "I say we call the girls and see if they want to go out tonight," he said with a determined look. "There's more than one way to get laid."

"What do you mean?" asked Travis.

"I mean we take the girls out for a hamburger and then go parking out by Clear Lake," said Melvin. "What you do in the back seat with Sara is none of my business, and you keep your nose out of the front seat."

"Well, what do you plan on doing?"

"What do you think?"

"You can't have sex with us in the back seat!"

"Why not?"

"That sounds disgusting! We'll hear everything that's going on!"

Melvin pulled over to the curb and stopped. "If you doing it right, you'll be too busy getting laid to know what I'm doing. Just trust me on this, will you?"

Travis looked away. "I don't know," he muttered.

"Stop worrying," said Melvin. "You'll do just fine."

◆◆◆

The sun was already low in the western sky when Melvin turned down a dirt road just outside of town. It was a narrow road with trees lining both sides. The early evening sunlight filtered through the trees casting yellow and orange spears of light across the road. They had already picked up Linda and were on their way to Sara's house.

"Hope you know where you're going," said Travis from the back seat.

"This is her place," said Melvin turning onto a drive partially hidden by the trees. It was a long drive that wound through the trees and stopped at a small ranch house. Melvin pulled up to the front door and sounded the horn.

"Jesus, that's rude," said Travis.

"What's rude?" asked Melvin.

"Honking the horn."

"How else did you figure on getting her attention?"

"I don't know. It just seems rude, that's all."

Melvin turned in his seat. "Do you have any idea how old-fashioned you are?"

Just then, the front door opened, and Sara bounced down the steps. "Hi, guys," she shouted as she climbed into the back seat. "Where are we going?"

Travis slid away from her. "We thought we'd go get a hamburger and a shake," he said his voice shaking.

Melvin turned the car around and started down the driveway. "Then, we thought we could go over by Clear Lake and have a little fun," he said reaching under the front seat. He pulled out a bottle of Vodka and held it up. "And this is just what the doctor ordered for having fun."

"That's my baby," said Linda with a smile.

Sara turned to Travis. "Sounds like we're going to have a great evening," she said sliding across the seat. She straightened a lock of hair that had fallen onto Travis' forehead. "You don't look too excited. Is there something wrong?"

"Not really," he said sitting straight in his seat.

"Come on," she prodded. "Something is wrong. I can tell it." Travis said nothing. He glanced at the bottle that Melvin was still waving in the air. "That's it! You've never had a drink, have you?"

"Yes, I have," he blurted. "I had one of my dad's beers once."

"Drinking one of your dad's beers is one thing," she said laughing aloud. "Eighty-proof liquor is entirely another. I once drank nearly a half of a bottle of that stuff at a party. I was drunk for a week."

Travis stared at the young woman sitting beside him. "You're so different tonight," he said with a puzzled look. "You seem a little wild."

"Wild!" shouted Sara with a smile. She shook her head sending her blond hair cascading over her shoulders. "I guess maybe I am a little wild. I just know I need to have a little fun. Do you ever have a time when you just need to blow off a little steam? Well, that's what I'm like right now. I need to blow off a little steam."

Travis folded his hands and placed them in his lap. He began to mutter. "I like to go for a walk when I feel like..."

"You know what?" she said leaning forward in her seat. "How 'bout we skip the hamburger and head straight for the lake?" Silence fell. Everyone looked at each other. "Come on. What are we waiting for?"

"I think she's got something there," said Melvin.

"Sounds great to me," said Linda.

All eyes turned to Travis. He forced a smile. "Sounds okay to me too," he said softly.

"Let's go!" shouted Melvin as he floored the accelerator.

It was nearly a twenty-minute ride over the back roads before they arrived at a small hill over looking the lake. It was already dark, and the only light was from the full moon. Melvin reached under the front seat and removed four paper cups. "You hold the cups while I pour," he said unscrewing the cap.

"You're nervous, aren't you?" asked Sara taking two cups of Vodka from Linda.

"Kinda," he said taking one of the cups from her. He stared into the cup and turned to Sara. "Here's looking at you," he said and took a sip. His body shuddered his eyes closed tight. "Jesus God!" he shouted. "What the hell is that?"

"There's one thing about it," she said taking a sip from her cup. "This will get ya where you want to go in a hurry."

Travis stared at his drink. "You're right about that," he said without looking up.

"So, what did you think of your first real drink?" she asked taking another sip.

Travis paused and then took another small sip. "I always wondered what this stuff tasted like. I can't believe people like the taste."

Sara gulped the rest of her drink. "I don't think anybody drinks this stuff for the taste," she said pouring herself another.

Travis stared into his cup. "I didn't think I'd ever drink this stuff. I still can't believe it."

The smile on Sara's face disappeared. "You seem upset," she said. "What's wrong?"

Travis leaned over and set the cup on the floor. "When I was a little kid, I loved my grandparents very much and spent as much time at their house as I could. They weren't rich or own some fancy house, but they were warm and wonderful people who made you feel right at home. I had heard rumors about my grandpa's drinking and how he would change almost like a Werewolf or Jekyl and Hyde. I didn't believe the rumors. I mean how could anyone as nice as my grandpa do something like that?

One day, I decided to spend the night at their place. I had never done anything like that before. I was so excited. I remember Grandma and I watched television that evening. Grandpa was at some kind of convention and was going to be late getting home. I could hardly wait for him to get there. It just didn't seem right with him not there."

Sara eased back in her seat and set her drink on the floor as well. "I thought your grandpa was your hero," she said.

"This is my other grandpa, my mother's father."

Travis paused and glanced out the window as the forgotten memories came back. "I remember hearing the back door open and thinking how everything was right in the world now that he was home. I had never seen anybody like that. I guess I was about as scared as I could be. He was all right at first just kind of laughing and carrying on. I knew something was wrong with him, but I had no idea what it was.

Then, it happened. Grandma said something about his drinking too much, and out of the blue he slugged her in the stomach. He caught her off guard, and the blow knocked the wind out of her. She fell to the floor, and while she struggled to breathe again, he hit her in the head with his fist.

I stood there dumbfounded not knowing what to do when all of a sudden he grabbed me by the arm, dragged me across the floor, and locked me up in a closet. I must have been in there for an hour until Grandma finally let me out. Grandpa had passed out on the floor. I remember stepping over him and thinking to myself that if this is what alcohol does to a person, there's no way I'll ever even think about drinking."

Sara took a deep breath and shifted in her seat.

Travis glanced at Sara. He could see that she was bothered by the story. "I'm sorry I told you that story. I didn't want to upset you."

"Oh, that's alright," she said leaning over and picking up her drink. She tossed it out the window paper cup and all. "We don't have to drink to have fun."

Travis smiled.

"By the way, what ever happened to your grandparents?" she asked.

"Grandma is still living. She's eighty years old," he said. "My grandpa was killed in a car accident."

"Was it drinking and driving?"

"Kind of," said Travis. "The only difference was my grandpa wasn't the one who had been drinking. The other guy was. Kinda ironic, don't you think?"

Sara said nothing. She turned and stared out the window.

It was completely dark outside now. A nearly full moon cast a soft gray light in the car. Melvin and Linda had disappeared below the front seat, and from the sounds they were making things were getting hot. Linda heard the sound of a zipper and turned to Travis. She smiled and slid over next to Travis.

"We don't need alcohol to have fun, do we?" she cooed.

Travis was wide-eyed. He eased back in his seat his hands trembling. "I don't know. What did you have in mind?"

Sara took his hand and began to play with his fingers. "What would you like to do?" she asked.

Travis turned and studied the young woman sitting next to him. Her smile was unlike anything he had ever seen. Instinctively, he knew that she wanted to make love to some degree or another. He wasn't quite sure how far she would want to go with two other people in the front seat. It seemed obvious from the sounds they were now making that just about anything would be acceptable with them.

He could feel his whole body trembling. He had never done anything like this. All he was sure of was that it was wrong for them to have sex, and that he needed to keep his wits about him.

His voice began to quiver. "I don't think it's such a good idea for us to get too involved."

Her smiled disappeared. Her face took on a pouty look her lips slightly parted. "You don't want to get involved with me. Is that what you said?" she asked still holding onto his hand.

"I didn't say that," he blurted. "I just meant we shouldn't …you know."

She leaned forward, her lips next to his. He started to press his lips against hers and suddenly stopped.

"It's just not right for us to do this," he announced.

Melvin's head popped over the seat. "I knew you'd blow it," he said with a laugh.

The softness in Sara's face disappeared. Her eyebrows furrowed as she glared at Travis. "You can't be serious!" she shouted. "You can't just start something like this and stop!"

Travis dropped his hands in his lap. "I'm sorry," he said. "I just can't do something like this. I really am sorry."

Sara sat motionless scowling at Travis. "Not half as sorry as I am," she barked. She leaned towards the front seat. "Melvin, would you be so kind as to take me home?"

Melvin lifted his head his hair was tossed and his eyes blurry. "You're kiddin'," he slurred.

"No, I'm not," she announced as she folded her arms and leaned back in the seat.

Melvin said nothing. He glanced down at Linda lying on the seat and then turned to Sara. "Do you know how close I was?" he muttered. As if it were a rhetorical question, no one answered. He pulled up his pants and turned in his seat. "Okay, we're dumping you guys off, and then Linda and I have something to take care of." He started the engine and slowly drove away.

Travis glanced out the window and then turned to Sara. "I really am sorry," he said softly.

Sara took a deep sigh. "I know I shouldn't be mad at you. In fact, I should respect what you did. Most guys would take advantage of the situation, and you didn't. That says a lot about you. I guess I was just in the mood. You know?"

"I'm sorry that I made you mad," he said with a soft voice.

"Oh, don't worry," she said with a slight smile. "I'll get over it."

Melvin sped down the back roads sending a cloud of dust high in the air behind them. He turned onto the road that went in front of Sara's house.

"Just let me out right here," she said abruptly. "I'll walk the rest of the way." Melvin brought the vehicle to a stop, and Sara opened the door. She paused and turned to Travis. Her face softened. "Call me tomorrow," she said and got out of the car.

"Good night," shouted Travis.

Sara turned and gave a quick wave and watched as the car drove away.

The evening had brought a chill to the air. The moon was bright that night casting dark and eerie shadows transforming the plush landscape into a colorless, black-and-white countryside. Sara could see the faint and distant lights from her house. She decided to take the shortcut, so she turned off the road and into the woods.

It was much darker in the woods than she imagined. The trees were dense, and the little moonlight that filtered through the leaves created dancing shadows in every direction. Sara had cut through the woods at night before, but tonight it was different. Tonight the woods did not seem as friendly. In fact, they seemed almost hostile. She was frightened. She did not know why. She just knew that she had a feeling, a feeling of danger.

Something was wrong. Sara had the deep sense that someone was near. She quickened her step the leaves from last autumn exploding under her feet. She came to an abrupt stop and listened. Footsteps probably fifty yards away came to a stop as well.

"Hello," she called out. "Is someone out there? Is that you, Travis?" She listened for a reply. Nothing. She peered into the darkness but could see nothing.

She turned and began to run stepping high to avoid the hazards of the underbrush and weaving in and around the trees. She glanced behind her but could see nothing. Maybe it was her imagination, but she was sure there was someone in the woods with her. She turned and looked behind her again, and without warning slammed into a tree. She fell to the ground and lay there motionless.

Moments passed. She sat upright on the ground and lightly touched her head. A small bump had already appeared, but there was no time for that. Someone was definitely following her. She could hear the footsteps, and they were closing fast. Her heart was pounding, her mouth dry. She got to her feet and stood by the tree. The footsteps stopped.

Dead silence. Sara knew that he was trying to locate her. She was sure that the pounding of her heart would give her away.

She turned to the house. The light from the kitchen window beckoned to her. The edge of the woods was only a few feet away, and beyond that was fifty yards of open ground to the front door. She turned her head and peered into the woods. She could see nothing. She turned back to the house and plotted a path that would take her through the trees and into the open.

Sara began to run. It was a slow pace to avoid the trees. Soon she was clear of the woods and began a full sprint to the house. She ran as fast as she could. Her lungs were on fire. It seemed like an eternity until she finally reached the front porch. She slid across the wooden floor up to the front door. She turned the handle. Nothing! The door was locked! She fumbled in her coat pocket for the key. No key! She searched the other pocket. Her body heaved as she gasped for air. Thank God! She found it! She tried desperately to insert the key into the lock. Her hand was shaking violently. She could hear the thunder of approaching footsteps. Sara held one hand with the other and finally mated the key with the lock. She swung the door open and slammed it behind her. She leaned against the door gasping for air. Her whole body was shaking. She slowed her breathing and pressed her ear to the door. Surely he must be on the porch by now. She could hear no sounds from outside. Where was he? He should be on the porch.

Then, it hit her. How could she have been so stupid? She raced down the hallway towards the back of the house. She locked all the windows in the bedrooms. She thought of how silly that was. All he needed to do was to break a window to get in.

She raced back to the kitchen. She stood in the middle of the room looking for a weapon. She had never owned a gun. Even the sight of a gun frightened her. She opened a drawer and grabbed a ten-inch butcher knife. She squeezed it tightly. It fit her hand perfectly. A feeling of confidence swept over her.

She returned to the center of the room. She needed something else. She knew she would not have the strength to fight a grown man. She needed an advantage. Her eyes scanned the kitchen. There had to be something she could use. Sara searched the cupboards looking for anything she might use to help her.

Finally, there it was! On the bottom shelf of the pantry were two gallons of pancake syrup leftover from some family get-together. She glanced back at the door that led to the rest of the house and the floor in front of it. She needed something to wedge between the door and the jamb. She searched the room until her eyes fell on a doorstop.

Sara heard the sound of glass breaking in a back bedroom. Just as she feared he was coming in through a window. She grabbed the doorstop and wedged it in the door. She needed a hammer to force the wedge deeper, and without even looking she knew that it was on the back porch. Instinctively, she pulled off one of her shoes and beat on the wedge.

More glass broke as the man fell through the window and on to the floor. Sara poured the maple syrup on the floor in front of the door. She picked up the knife and held it tightly in her trembling hand. This was it. She knew it. Her hands trembled as she reached over and turned off the light. Everything was ready.

Sara heard approaching footsteps. She could feel her heart pounding her whole body was throbbing. The intruder stopped at the door. He tried pushing on it but no luck. Suddenly, the door flew open as he rammed it with his shoulder. His momentum carried him into the kitchen. He found himself in the middle of a pool of syrup with his feet skating in different directions. He fell to the floor. Sara knew that it was time. She had to do it. This was a case of self-defense, and she needed to act now.

She snapped on the kitchen light and stared at the man on the floor. "Harlan Steelman!" she shouted. "I should have known!"

Harlan stopped his struggle to get up when he looked up to see the knife in her outstretched hand. She bent down and lunged the knife at the man. He rolled over, and the knife missed its mark. Sara lost her balance and fell to her knees with Harlan knocking the knife from her hand. It slid across the floor and disappeared under the stove. The young woman scrambled to her feet and started for the door. Harlan grabbed her by the ankle. He had a tight grip, and she screamed from the pain. She scanned the room looking for something to use as a weapon. There on the stove was an iron skillet. She stretched until she was able to grab the cooking utensil.

Sara swung the skillet behind her and caught Harlan in the side of the head. It made a deadening sound and sent him reeling across the floor releasing his grip. She bolted across the floor, opened the door, and ran into the night.

Holding his head with both hands Harlan screamed, "You bitch! I'll get you for this!" He pulled his hands away to find them covered in blood. He got on his knees and crawled across the floor until he was clear of the syrup. He got slowly to his feet still reeling from the blow to his head and headed into the night.

Harlan stopped just outside the door. He could hear fading footsteps running down the driveway.

Sara knew that if she could just make it to the main road she would surely find a passing motorist and get help.

Then, it happened. The main road was in sight and to save time, Sara cut through a small patch of trees. It was dark, and she did not see the abandoned bicycle lying in the ditch beside the road. Her foot caught in the spokes of the wheel, and she came crashing to the ground her head hitting a rock at the side of the road.

Harlan stopped in the middle of the road. He glanced both ways and could see nothing. It was quiet that night. Not even the night sounds of summer could be heard. He began walking down the middle of the road searching from side-to-side.

There she was lying face down in the road. Harlan glanced up and down the road and peered into the dark forest. He knelt down beside her and gently rolled her over. In the moonlight he could see blood pouring from a cut in her head. His hand moved slowly down her body following every contour. He then pulled up her skirt revealing her soft femininity. He ran his hand over her soft inner thighs and then into her silk panties. His whole body seemed to throb with passion.

Harlan stood straight and began to unbuckle his belt when suddenly he heard a growling. He spun in the road. There standing in the middle of the road was a large animal shaped like a dog. Harlan stepped back. Two eyes pierced the darkness with an eerie glow. Its teeth were bared, and it was moving slowly towards him. Harlan eased back several steps, turned, and ran down the road.

Jake Brown walked slowly into the waiting room. He straightened the magazines and emptied the trash. It wasn't his job, but he liked to keep the room looking neat. He always figured the people who were there had enough problems and didn't need to see a mess.

Jake had been the security guard at the Community Hospital for nearly thirty years. He hadn't always worked the graveyard shift. In fact, he was hired for days. Five years later, he's asked to fill in for someone on nights, and that's where he stayed.

It was after 10:00. Jake walked slowly over to the Admittance Desk. "I'm going outside for a smoke break. If you need me just give me a call," he said patting the walkie-talkie clipped to his belt. He walked outside and took a deep breath. The crisp night air felt good after being inside. He pulled a cigarette from his shirt pocket and lit it up. He expelled a lung-full of smoke and watched as it disappeared into the dark sky.

Suddenly, Jake leaned forward and peered into the darkness. In the distance he could see the outline of a man carrying something. He was nearly at the hospital door before he realized that it was Lone Wolf, and he was carrying a woman who appeared to be unconscious.

Jake ran inside, grabbed a gurney, and wheeled it outside. Very gently, Lone Wolf laid the young woman down and slowly stepped back. He stared at the young woman for a moment, glanced at Jake, and disappeared into the night.

CHAPTER 7

Sheriff Miller fired down the drink in front of him and slammed the empty glass on the bar. An overweight man in a white apron picked up a bottle of Jim Bean and refilled the glass.

"So, what the hell is the matter with you?" asked the bartender. "I can't remember the last time I saw you drinking like this before noon."

The Sheriff picked up the glass and stared at it. "It's Lone Wolf," he announced as he sipped from the glass. "Looks like I'm going to have to bring him in. Seems like he's the one who brought in the little Simmons girl. Dropped her right at the back door of the hospital. Can you imagine that?"

"What makes you think he hurt her?" asked the bartender. "Seems to me that anyone who would do something like that wouldn't take the time to carry her two miles to the hospital."

"How long have you known me, Frank?" asked the Sheriff. "Have you ever known me to arrest a man who was innocent? I've had my eye on that Lone Wolf character for a long time. He's guilty. I can smell it. Besides, they found a hair from a wild animal such as a Lone Wolf on her. Guess where they found it?" Frank said nothing. "They found it lying on her panties. That proves that he was up to no good. He had to have had her dress up. How else would that hair have got there?"

Frank picked up a rag and wiped the bar near the Sheriff's glass. "Maybe her dress was already pulled up when he got there," he said. "Besides, a wild animal hair doesn't convict Lone Wolf. It's never been proven that he actually turns into an animal."

The sheriff gulped his drink and set the glass on the bar. "How come all of a sudden you're sticking up for the Lone Wolf? That seems mighty strange to me."

"I ain't sticking up for anybody," he said indignantly. "Just seems to me you've already got him tried and convicted. I don't think that big dumb Indian has ever hurt a soul, and what you got on him damn sure won't hold up in court."

"You know sometimes I think you missed your calling," said the Sheriff. "I think you should have been a lawyer. You're a big enough pain in the ass to be one." He swung around on his stool and got to his feet. "Why don't you close up and come with me. I need to bring him in for questioning."

"You know something," said Frank taking off his apron and dropping it on the bar. "I think I will. After all, somebody has to stick up for the man. God knows he won't get a fair shake from you."

On the other side of town a young man sat quietly on his front porch. His feet dangled over the side just reaching the ground. He had swung his feet back and forth enough that he had dug a small ditch in the dirt. He felt badly about what had happened the night before. It seemed the right thing to do at the time, but now he wasn't so sure. They both wanted sex. That was certain, so why did he refuse her? He hoped it was because of his morals and not because of his timidity around girls. He also hoped that she would forgive him, but he knew that there was a good chance she would never date him again.

Just as he got to his feet a red convertible came to a stop in front of his house. A young man leaned out the window. "Travis, come over here! Quick!" said Melvin motioning with his arm.

"What's wrong?" asked Travis walking over to the car.

"You don't know, do ya?"

"Know what?"

Melvin took a deep breath. "Last night when we dropped off Sara someone attacked her!"

"Oh, my God!" Travis exclaimed. "Is she alright?"

"I don't know," said Melvin. "She's in the hospital."

"Would you take me over there?" asked Travis.

"They won't let you see her," said Melvin. "She's in Intensive Care, besides we have another problem."

"What's that?"

"The Sheriff thinks Lone Wolf did it."

"How did he get that idea?"

Melvin ran his fingers through his hair. "It seems that Lone Wolf was the one who carried her all the way from Sara's place into town. Must be two miles or more. Anyway, since he was the last one seen with her I guess they figure he must have done it."

Travis glanced away. "You know as well as I do that he didn't do it. What do we do now?"

"My guess is that the Sheriff is on his way out to get Lone Wolf," said Melvin. "If you were to get your ass in this car, we could beat it out there and find him before the Sheriff does. You know he has no idea where to look." Travis stood motionless. "Well, are you coming or not?"

Melvin took the back way through town and into the country stopping at the edge of the woods just outside of town. They jumped the fence and picked their way through the dense undergrowth until they were standing at the door of a small shack.

"Lone Wolf!" called Melvin. "Where ever you are, we need to talk with you!"

"Why is it whenever we come here he's never around, and then suddenly he appears?" asked Travis.

"I don't know," said Melvin. "But we don't have much time. If he's going to appear he needs to do it right now."

"Is the Sheriff coming?" asked Travis. The two boys turned and searched the woods in the direction of the road.

They both jumped at the sound of a voice from behind them. "What you want?" asked Lone Wolf his deep voice resonating.

"Jesus Christ!" shouted Travis. "Don't scare me like that!"

"You jumpy," said Lone Wolf dropping a dead rabbit on a tree stump. "What wrong with you two?"

Travis paused. He searched the area behind the big man standing in front of him. "How in the hell do you do that?"

"How do I do what?" asked Lone Wolf.

"Suddenly appear out of nowhere like that. That just ain't normal."

Lone Wolf smiled. He said nothing.

"Come on, let's get going," said Melvin taking a step. "We don't have time for this."

"What is troubling you?" asked Lone Wolf.

"The Sheriff is on his way over here right now to take you to jail for attacking Sara Simmons," said Travis.

His smile disappeared. He stared blankly at the two boys until a look of understanding swept over his face. "That the little girl I found in the road last night, isn't it?" he asked.

"That's her," said Travis. "Now, let's get going."

Lone Wolf grabbed Travis by the arm. "She your girlfriend?"

"I guess you might say that," said Travis. "I don't know. Some would say that we're anything but friends."

"You don't ask me if I did this thing. Why?"

Travis glanced at Melvin and then back to the big man in front of him. "You're not the kind of person who would do such a thing. It's as simple as that."

Lone Wolf smiled. "You good friend."

"You two want to break this up?" asked Melvin. "We need to get out of here."

"I not go," said Lone Wolf. "I stay here."

"You can't stay here," said Travis. "The Sheriff will be here any minute. He's going to lock you up in jail. You don't want that to happen, do you?"

"I do nothing wrong."

"That's fine and dandy, but the Sheriff thinks you did," said Travis. Lone Wolf said nothing. His lips tightened. "Look, you're not going to do anybody any good sittin' in jail. At least, if you out you might be able to do something to clear your name."

Lone Wolf stopped. He turned in the direction of the road. "Okay, but where will I hide?"

Travis turned to Melvin.

"My folks are out of town for the next few days," said Melvin. "He can stay at my place." Each glanced at the others as if waiting for a cue.

"Then, let's get going!" said Travis.

It was a short ride into town, but today, Melvin drove slow enough so as not to attract attention. With Lone Wolf lying on the floor in the back seat, Melvin drove all the back roads and alleys until he turned onto the long driveway leading to his house. Once inside he dropped the garage door, and the three got out of the car.

It was a white two-story colonial, nearly four thousand square feet in size and considered to be one of the more prominent in town. Melvin led the way through a side door and into the kitchen.

Lone Wolf stepped inside the kitchen his eyes searching in amazement. "This nice house, but so big outside and so small inside."

Melvin gave a puzzled look to Travis. "Oh, now I know what you mean," he said with a smile. "You don't understand. This is just the kitchen. There are other rooms just beyond that doorway," he said pointing across the room.

Lone Wolf gazed at the open doorway and then returned to his search of the kitchen. "This some place," he said walking slowly across the floor stopping at the refrigerator.

"I don't think this was such a good idea," said Melvin.

"Why?" asked Travis with a smile.

"Does the phrase, 'A bull in a china shop' come to mind?"

"How much damage can a six-foot seven-inch Indian do?"

"I smell fresh kill," said Lone Wolf his nose pressed against the door.

"Here, let me show you," said Melvin opening the refrigerator door.

Lone Wolf jumped. He stared in amazement. "Look at all that food," he said. "We eat food. It go bad in that box."

"Stick your hand in there," said Melvin. Lone Wolf pulled back. "Go on, stick it in there. It won't hurt you."

Slowly and cautiously, Lone Wolf thrust his hand into the lighted box. He turned and smiled. "It cold in here. How you capture that cold air?"

Melvin pulled the Indian's hand out and closed the door. "Come here," he said walking across the room. He stopped in front of the stove and turned on one of the burners. "Hold your hand over that."

The big man cautiously held his hand over the burner that was now beginning to glow a bright red with heat. He quickly pulled his hand back. "That like campfire," he said holding his hand.

Melvin reached over and turned off the burner. "I guess you could call it that," he said with a smile. "Our own campfire in a box."

Lone Wolf scanned the room. "I like kitchen," he said. "This is where I stay."

Melvin pointed at the stove. "Now, you know, Lone Wolf, you can't touch any of these knobs. Do you understand?"

Lone Wolf turned the knob that Melvin had used. The burner started to glow again. "I like kitchen. I live here."

Melvin turned to Travis. "Boy, this was a great idea. I can see the headlines now, 'Indian dies in house fire. Body found slumped over stove.' How do I get in these messes?"

Lone Wolf walked over to the sink. He bent over and examined the faucet. "This makes water," he said playing with the spout. "I saw this in town. How does it work?"

Melvin turned the handle, and water splashed out. Lone Wolf jumped, smiled, and thrust his hand back under the stream. "So many things you white people have, this is the best."

Melvin glanced at Travis. "Of all the things we have, and you think water from a faucet is the best. Why is that?"

The big man leaned back, and with his other hand he caught the water as it dripped from his fingers. He then bent over and sucked it from his palm. The smile disappeared from his face as he wiped his hands on his shirt. "Have you ever drank from river and see dead fish floating by?"

Silence followed.

Melvin walked over to the kitchen table. "Let's sit down," he said pulling out one of the chairs. "Lone Wolf, you once said that's not your real name. Are you ready to tell us your name?"

He took a seat at the table still studying the kitchen. "You not believe when I tell you."

Travis smiled. "I knew it was going to be juicy," he said. "It's something like Lone Wolf With Boner, isn't it?"

Melvin laughed. "Come on, Lone Wolf. It's time. Tell us your real name."

Lone Wolf shifted his weight in the chair. He first looked at Travis, then Melvin, then smiled. "My real name John Smith," he announced.

The two boys glanced at each other. "John Smith!" shouted Travis. "You can't be serious! How did you ever get a name like that?"

Lone Wolf kept his smile, but it was somehow different. It was a smile of pain. "My father gave me that name. He thought it was time we become like the white man. He thought that name help me to be more like your people. He saw the future belonging to the white man. Have much respect for your people. He was a wise man, but not sure this good idea."

"Why?" asked Travis.

"Everyone have same reaction. Think it funny."

"What ever happened to your father?"

Lone Wolf turned and glanced out the window. "He hanged by the neck on a tree," he said his face like stone. "I watched as group of men in white sheets dragged him off one night to a tall oak tree. I remember it so tall man must throw rope many times to get it over branch. I just small boy not sure what they doing. I remember thinking that rope must be evil thing. I think maybe if they are unable to get rope over branch they let my father go. I tried to get to my father, but one man hold me back. I look down and see white hands holding me.

Finally, rope sail over branch, and they slip noose around my father's neck. It's then I figured what they were going to do. I screamed and yelled and struggled to get free, but man too strong.

I stopped my struggle and look at my father. He stands erect and proud. His eyes searched the crowd until they find me. He stares at me. I remember his eyes. They were strong and brave. He smiled at me. I'll never forget that smile as long as I live. It was the smile that said everything would be all right.

They hung a man that day all those years ago, but they didn't kill the spirit. His spirit still lives in me."

Silence followed. It was an awkward silence as the two boys fought for words to say. Lone Wolf got to his feet and walked over to a window. He leaned against the pane as memories of better times came rushing back.

Travis stared at the big man. He could feel his pain and tried to imagine the horror of that night. It seemed so unfair to take that man's life in such a brutal way and even more unfair to allow his son to watch.

Melvin slapped his hands together as if to break the silence. "I'm starved. Let's eat."

Travis flashed him a look of disgust. His actions seemed disrespectful.

"What?" said Melvin his hands open wide. "Don't give me that look. It's time to eat. Now, what do you want?" He got out of his chair and opened the refrigerator. "Guess what? I got a half of a pizza in here from last night. I'll just nuke them in the microwave, and we've got lunch." He set the pizza on the kitchen counter and turned to Lone Wolf. "Have you ever had pizza before?"

Lone Wolf turned and said nothing. He returned to his seat as he stared at the food.

Melvin put two slices on a small plate and stuck them in the oven. He pushed some buttons and it soon began to hum. Lone Wolf leaned closer. He tried to see through the darkened window. Suddenly, the timer went off, and Lone Wolf jumped back. Melvin opened the door and removed the food. He slid it across the table stopping in front of Lone Wolf.

"Watch out! It's hot!" said Melvin.

The big man, cautiously, lowered his finger until it was touching the food. He brought his finger to his mouth and licked the warm sauce. He smacked his lips as he stared at the food. Once again, he dipped his finger in the sauce and licked it clean. "Pizza good. I like pizza," he said.

"Pick up a piece and eat it," said Travis.

He thrust a piece into his mouth and tore half of it off. "That pizza real good. How you get it?"

"Just call up Angelo's, and twenty minutes later it's at the front door."

"Someone bring it to your house?"

"Beats picking it up yourself," said Melvin. "Of course, this way costs you a buck for a tip."

Lone Wolf finished the slice as he stared at Melvin with a blank look. "How does pizza get hot? What is that?" he asked pointing at the microwave oven.

"That's a nuke machine," said Melvin. "Microwave oven."

"How does it work?"

"Don't know. Makes things hot in a hurry though. That's all I care about. So, how do you like your first pizza?"

Lone Wolf picked up the other piece and stuck half of it in his mouth. "Pizza good. They deliver to my place in the woods?"

Melvin laughed. "I don't think so, Chief."

"That too bad. I really like pizza."

The smile on Melvin's face disappeared. "I'll tell you what, Lone Wolf, Travis and I have some things to take care of.

Grab the rest of that pizza over there, and we'll set you up in front of the TV while we're gone," said Melvin walking out of the kitchen and into the living room.

Lone Wolf followed carrying the sagging, grease-soaked box. His mouth dropped open as he entered the living room. It was a large, spacious room with vaulted ceilings, and one end was all glass overlooking a wooded backyard. In the center of the room was a large projection television.

"Sit down on the couch, Lone Wolf, and I'll introduce you to the greatest invention of all, the remote control," said Melvin. The big man took his place in the center of the L-shaped sofa. Melvin handed him a small box. "Here, this is called the white man's monument to laziness. See these two buttons. They change the channel. These two make the sound go up or down, and that's about all there is to it."

Lone Wolf pressed one of the buttons, and the picture changed. He jumped, and then a smile slowly spread across his face. "This good. I've seen these in town not sure what they are. What you call this?"

"This is called a TV," said Travis.

Lone Wolf changed channels again. "I like TV," he said.

"Well, have fun," said Travis. "We'll be back later."

The two boys started for the door. Travis glanced over his shoulder. Lone Wolf was picking up a slice of pizza with one hand and changing channels with the remote control in his other. "Where are we going?" he asked.

"To the hospital," replied Melvin. "Let's go check on Sara. I think we both know that guy in there didn't do anything to her except carry her to the hospital. This whole thing smells like Uncle Harlan."

◆◆◆

At the edge of town, a young woman lightly taps on the screen door of the Steelman farmhouse. She peers into the dark interior but can see nothing. "Nolan," she calls out. She, cautiously, opens the door and lets herself in. She searches the dark living room, but there is no sign of the old man. She had arrived later than usual, and by this time of day, Nolan Steelman would have been sitting in his favorite chair finishing his first pack of cigarettes.

Kara sensed that something was wrong. "Mr. Steelman!" she softly shouted. She listened for a reply or a stirring of some kind. Nothing. Kara walked slowly into the kitchen. It seemed pointless to fix a meal for the man if he wasn't home, but where was he? It wasn't like him not to be home. He probably was called away on business and had no time to leave word for her. Maybe he died in his sleep. He could be upstairs at that very moment his body decaying in the summer heat.

Suddenly, the front screen door opened wide and slammed shut. She heard someone trip and fall on the floor. "Shit!" she heard someone say. "Goddamn run down place!" Fear struck Kara. She knew that voice. Staggering footsteps came closer.

"Honey, I'm home!" shouted Harlan leaning against the doorway to the kitchen. His clothes were soaked with alcohol and covered with dirt. Still clutching an empty bottle of beer, he reeled uncontrollably nearly falling again to the floor.

"Where's Nolan?" asked Kara.

Harlan smiled. He flattened his hand and swooped it back and forth. "He took a plane to somewhere. He didn't tell me where he was going."

"When is he coming home?"

"Not 'til tomorrow morning," said Harlan leaning against the wall. "That means that you and I got all night together. What do you think about that?"

Kara started for the door. "I think you're drunk, and I'm going home."

Harlan stepped in the doorway blocking her way. "And why would you want to go home to that worthless husband of yours. It's my guess he hasn't got it up in years. You know how I can tell? I can tell from how sexually frustrated you are."

Kara stopped in front of Harlan. "Let me through that doorway," she said with a stern voice.

"Oh, come on, you little sweet thing, I think the time is right for you to be nice to old Harlan," he said grabbing her shoulders.

Kara slipped from his grasp and stepped back. "Harlan, please step aside so I can go home."

"I don't think so," said Harlan his arms outstretched. "I think today is the day we settle up on old debts. What do you think about that?"

Kara crouched down and started for the door. Harlan grabbed her with both hands and threw her to the floor. Before she could get her footing, he straddled her with his feet and sat down on top of her pinning her to the floor.

"Let me go!" she screamed.

Harlan grabbed her blouse and jerked it open sending buttons across the floor. He then ripped off her bra and threw it across the room. He smiled as he stared at her firm breasts saliva dripping from his mouth and puddling on her stomach.

"Harlan, you bastard, let me up!" she screamed.

His smile disappeared. "Shut the hell up, bitch! Who the hell do you think you are?"

Kara struggled. "Harlan, you low-life bastard, let me go right now!"

Harlan's teeth clenched. "Shut the fuck up! Do you hear me?"

"You let me go right now, or I swear to God I'll see you rot in hell!"

Harlan reached back and slapped the woman in the face. He grabbed her by the neck with both hands and lightly squeezed. "You fucking bitch! I ought to choke the stinking life out of you. I could, you know. I could snap your neck like a pretzel." Kara froze. She stared wide-eyed at the man leaning over her. "Hell, I could have finished off that little bitch last night. I would have too if it hadn't been for that goddamn Indian."

Suddenly, Harlan's face went blank. He released his grip on her neck and sat up straight. "Damn, I don't feel so good," he said holding his head with both hands. His head was spinning. He reeled from side-to-side. "Damn," he muttered.

Kara stopped her struggle. She watched in horror as this man spun out of control. There was no place for her to go, and nothing she could do.

Then, it happened. Harlan leaned over and heaved onto the floor just missing Kara's head. A white, milky substance splattered her face. Harlan stood up his feet still straddling the woman below and wiped his mouth with his sleeve.

This was her chance. With all her strength she swung her foot crashing it in Harlan's crotch.

"Jesus God!" he screamed. Grabbing himself with both hands he fell on to the floor. "My dear God help me!" he shouted rolling back-and-forth across the floor.

Kara scrambled to her feet and ran out of the house.

◆◆◆

In a small ranch house at the edge of town, a man stepped down from his stepladder. John set his paintbrush on the rim of the paint can. He leaned back and admired the freshly painted ceiling. All his life, John had been good with his hands. There wasn't a home improvement project he couldn't do, but painting was one thing he preferred not to do. He smiled as he stared at his work. "Not too bad," he muttered aloud.

Suddenly, the front door burst open, and Kara collapsed onto a kitchen chair. She bent over as she gasped for air. John ran into kitchen and stopped in front his wife. She got to her feet and fell into his arms. "Oh, John, it was just horrible!" she cried into his shoulder.

John pushed her back at arm's length. Her hair was mussed, and her blouse was torn exposing her breasts. "My God, Kara, what happened?"

"Harlan Steelman!" she shouted. "The bastard tried to rape me!"

John's expression changed from shock to anger. "Are you all right? Do you want me to take you to the hospital?"

"No, I'm okay," she replied. "I'm just a little shook up, I guess." She eased herself back into the chair. "He was too drunk to really do anything."

"Did he rape you?" asked John bending down.

"No, not really," she said. "He started out like he was going to, but he got sick. When he stood up, I kicked him in the nuts. I think I got him pretty good too because when I left he was still rolling on the floor."

John stood up and took a deep breath. "Are you sure you're all right?"

"Just a little scared, that's all."

"Where did this happen? At the farm?"

"Yes."

"Kara, I want you to wait here," he said turning to the door. "I'm going to go pay a visit to Harlan Steelman. He's been a pain in my ass for much too long."

"Oh, please don't, John," said Kara getting to her feet. "Something bad is going to happen. I just know it. Please don't go over there."

"I have to, Kara," he said opening the door. "What kind of man would I be if I let him get away with that? Besides, he's needed an ass-kickin' ever since I've known him, and today's the day he gets one." He closed the door after him and stared at his wife through the screen. "You stay here. Do you hear me?"

"Please be careful, John."

He paused for a moment, turned, and marched off.

◆◆◆

Dark clouds lay low in the western sky as a summer storm approached. An older model station wagon turned onto a dirt road leaving billowing clouds of dust behind. John was enraged his teeth clenched tightly as he gripped the steering wheel with both hands. He turned down a long dirt drive that led to the Steelman farm and came to a stop at the front door.

Harlan snubbed out the cigarette he was smoking and got to his feet. He started across the living room when the front screen door exploded. John stopped in the middle of the floor. He stared at the man standing in front of him his fists clenched tightly. "All right, Harlan, you know what I'm here for. Let's do it," he said calmly.

Harlan set down the beer he was holding and held up his fists. "I've been waiting for this for a long time," he said. "I'm going to hurt you, John. Hurt you bad."

"Stop talking about it and do it," he said crouching in a fighting stance.

The two men circled in the center of the room their eyes fixed on each other. Harlan jabbed, and John darted to one side. "Nice move," said Harlan with a smile. He struck again. This time John deflected his blow with his arm and then slammed his right fist into Harlan's midsection. He buckled over gasping for air. John stepped back, pulled back his right fist, and with all his power caught Harlan in the face. Blood splattered as he reeled back and fell onto the floor.

Blood pouring from his mouth he scrambled to his feet. A look of panic swept over his face as he stared at his opponent. He searched the room for a weapon. There on the end table was a glass ashtray. He picked it up and threw it at John catching him in the middle of the forehead. John reeled and fell on the floor. As he started to lift himself off the floor, Harlan took two steps and kicked John in the head. He then kicked him again and again.

Harlan looked down at his blood-soaked boot and realized the damage he had inflicted. He stepped back gasping for air. Blood poured from his face as John lifted himself off the floor. He got to his knees and stared at his opponent. Harlan laughed. "You ain't got no business messin' with a junkyard dog," he said pointing at John. "I told you I'd kick your ass, and I meant it!" He took two strides and pulled back his leg when suddenly from a crouch position, John leaped at his assailant. Wrapping his arms around him, the two men fell to the floor rolling until they hit the sofa. John found himself on top. He straddled the man with his legs and began to pummel him with his fists. He hit him and hit him until he stopped struggling.

John got to his feet and stood over man lying on the floor. Harlan groaned. He was unrecognizable. John coughed up mucous and expelled it into Harlan's bloody face. "Fuck you," he muttered and walked out the door.

◆◆◆

The next morning brought sunlight streaming through the dirt-stained window. John rolled over in bed and groaned as he grabbed his head with both hands. His head ached as he tenderly touched his face. From the size of it he was sure that it was bruised and swollen. He got out of bed and walked across the bedroom. He sat down at a table and picked up a small mirror that belonged to his wife.

"Oh, my God," he muttered as he stared at his beaten face. Both eyes had been blackened, and the right side of his face was swollen and had turned a deep shade of purple. John dropped the mirror on the table and turned to the clock on the wall. It was after nine o'clock and Kara hadn't awakened him. She must have decided to let him sleep in this morning. She probably considered it good therapy for his injuries.

John turned and stared out the window. In the backyard to the house next to them two small boys threw a baseball back-and-forth. He watched as one of the boys took a big league windup before throwing the ball. He could feel the youthful energy, the desire to succeed, and even the dream for athletic prowess. He smiled as the ball slipped through a glove and dribbled into the neighbor's yard.

John turned and again picked up the mirror. He studied his eyes and the uninjured side of his face. Lines of age accented his facial features that already seemed to sag from the extra weight he carried. "My God, I'm getting old," he whispered aloud.

He looked past the mirror and focussed on a crack that ran aimlessly across the wall. His eyes blurred as his mind raced back to a time of his youth. His father crouched down and held up a catcher's mitt for a target. "All right, son," he would say. "Give me your fast ball." John leaned over and stared at the mitt his sixteen-year-old body twitching like a spring ready to be released. He took his windup and fired the ball. It cracked as it slammed into his father's leather glove. "That a boy! They can't hit what they can't see." John smiled.

"You're awake," said Kara walking into the room. "How do you feel?"

"What?" he asked blinking as if he had just awakened.

"How do you feel?"

"Like a truck ran over me."

Kara leaned over and examined his face. "Doesn't look good, but I think you'll live," she said. "How did Harlan look when you were done?"

John lightly touched his face. "The only difference between us is I'm standing and he wasn't."

"You didn't kill him, did you?"

"No such luck," said John. "He was moving when I left him."

Kara walked over and sat on the edge of the bed. "John, what are we going to do now? It just seems like everything we do turns out wrong. I know it felt good to beat up Harlan, but you know as well as I that it's only going to get worse. He's not going to let this go, and you know it."

John turned to Kara. "I was just thinking the same thing, and I say we get out of this town. We need a fresh start in a town where there are no Harlan Steelman's."

"Oh, John, you promised this would be our last move."

"I know, Kara, but I had no idea it was going to be like this."

"Maybe, Harlan will leave us alone now."

"No, Kara," said John. "It's only going to get worse. Like you said, he's not going to let this go. We need to get out of here. We need a clean start, and you know it. Now, what do you say?"

Kara glanced down at the floor. "I suppose you're right," she said softly. "I'm just tired. That's all. I want a home just like everyone else, and I don't think that's asking too much."

John got to his feet and walked across the room. "We're going to be all right," he said sitting down next to her. "You'll see." He reached over and took her hand in his. He leaned over and kissed her on the cheek when the doorbell rang. Kara jumped up and went to the door. In a few moments she returned with Sheriff Miller following behind her.

Still in his pajamas, John got to his feet. "Sheriff, what brings you over here? He asked.

"John, I need you to get your clothes on and come with me," said the Sheriff.

"What's the problem, Sheriff?" asked John.

The Sheriff took a deep breath. "I'm taking you in for the murder of Harlan Steelman."

CHAPTER 8

In an older neighborhood on the other side of town, a red Porsche convertible turned down a dirt road that ran next to the railroad tracks. It stopped in front of a small older ranch-style house that was the last house before the town dump. A young man in a bright green three-piece suit climbed out of his car and started for the front door. He stopped short at the sidewalk and read a newly posted sign: Murphy Collins, Attorney At Law. He shook his head and started for the door. A rusted motor from a 1978 Ford Granada sat proudly among the weeds in the front yard, and the trunk lid from the same vehicle leaned against the front of the house.

He was a tall African-American with cocoa skin, baby-faced features, and a slight, yet, warm smile that disarmed everyone he ever met. He stepped onto the concrete blocks that became the front porch, and moved aside the wooden screen door that leaned against the front door. He started to knock but soon discovered the front door was ajar. "Murph," he called out as he closed the door behind him. The living room had a sofa and a floor lamp. Heavy, dark drapes were drawn allowing in only the smallest amount of light. "Murphy, where are you?" he called out. He walked across the floor and opened the door to the only bedroom. Plywood had been nailed over the windows to keep light out. The young man flipped the light switch. A fully clothed man lay face down across the bed. Piles of dirty clothes lay on the floor, and empty beer cans were strewn over the room.

Murphy groaned and rolled over on the beer-stained bedspread sending a half-empty bottle of Vodka falling to the floor. "Who the hell?" he started to say as he squinted into the open doorway. "Is that you, Stu?" he asked grabbing his head.

"It's Stewart, you numbskull," he replied. "I wish you wouldn't call me Stu. It sounds like some kind of food that the likes of you eat. My God, man, what in Heaven's name happened here?"

Murphy quickly scanned the room. "What are you talking about?"

"This room!" he shouted. "Just look at it! It's a God-awful mess! I trust the patrons of your party had a good time. From the number of empty beer cans lying about, I'd say you had a house full of people."

Murphy glanced around the room. He turned to the man standing in front of him. "What party?" he asked with a puzzled look.

Stewart studied the room. "I don't think I've ever seen your bedroom. Is the way it always looks?"

"Pretty much, and why would you ever see my bedroom?"

"I can't imagine," he said. "So far it's been an experience I can live without."

Murphy swung his feet around and sat on the edge of the bed. He was a young man still in his twenties tall and skinny with a large stomach that stretched his shirts. With both hands he began to massage the sides of his head. "You know what, Stu? I'm in no mood for your crap this morning. What are you doing over here anyhow?"

"It's Stewart," he said. "My name is Stewart."

"What do you want, for Christ's sakes," said Murphy starting for the door.

"I have good news," said Stewart following behind.

Murphy stopped at the kitchen stove and picked up the coffeepot. "I need a cup of coffee. Want some?" he asked pouring a thick, black liquid into a cup.

"It's cold!"

Murphy gulped from the cup. "So what?"

"No one drinks cold coffee."

"Yes, they do."

"Who drinks cold coffee?"

Murphy glanced at the cup in his hand. He held out his arms and shrugged "Need I say more," he said taking another drink.

"I'm talking about normal people, everyday garden variety people not lunatics like you."

Murphy sat down at the kitchen table. "Come on, Stu, what's your good news?"

Stewart stared at the table. It was covered with empty beer cans and food encrusted plates. He pulled out a chair and with two fingers picked up a pair of women's panties. "Is this what you wear behind closed doors?" he asked dropping them on the floor.

"Jesus! Will you tell me what the good news is?"

"I think I've lined you up a murder case."

"A murder case? What are you talking about?"

Stewart glanced out the window. "Do you realize that new sign you stuck outside there is illegal?"

Murphy glanced outside. "What's wrong with it?"

"There's nothing actually wrong with the sign. It's the fact that you are running a business in a residential area. They have zoning laws about things like that."

"Since when has that become illegal?"

"Since Man discovered he didn't like living next to a factory."

Murphy paused. "I'll be darn," he muttered.

"You scare me, Murph," he said sitting down at the table. "You really do. You're a lawyer, and yet you say things like that. How in the hell did I ever get mixed up with someone like you?"

Murphy gulped his coffee. "What do you do anyhow? I see you sniffing around here from time-to-time, but what is your real function in life?"

"I'm a detective, for Christ's sakes, Murphy. I do your dirty work for you and never get paid for it, I might add. I'm your bitch. I'm your gopher. I generally take your crap and hope that someday I might get paid."

Murphy stopped and turned to the man sitting at the table. "My God, man," he said. "You sound like my ex-wife! Now, what's this about a murder case?"

"Some guy is in jail for murdering Harlan Steelman, and I'm positive that you're getting the case."

Murphy smiled. "Let me guess. You got a call from your brother, the Judge, and you told him that Murphy is ready to sit at the big folks' table. Stewart, you're my new best friend."

Stewart sat up straight. "You're calling me Stewart. My my. The man is delirious."

Murphy ran his fingers through his hair. "So, Harlan Steelman got whacked. Hell, they should give the guy a medal. Who did it, any way?"

"Some guy named John Watson," said Stewart. "Can't afford a lawyer. He doesn't even have a job which is where you come in."

Murphy stared past Stewart. "This could be my lucky break, you know. You can't get rich defending traffic tickets." Murphy paused, blinked his eyes, and turned to his friend. "Which reminds me, do you have a couple bucks you can loan me? They're going to turn off my electricity if I don't give them some money. They're funny that way."

Stewart reached for his wallet. "Loan is a word that people use when they plan to pay the money back. Why are you using that word?" he asked handing him a fifty-dollar bill.

Murphy picked up the bill and stared at it. He held out his hand. "This pays for the juice I used last month. Let's take care of this month too."

Stewart dug into his wallet and handed him another bill. "My God, man, don't you have any humility? You take a handout like I owed it to you."

Murphy stopped and glared at the man in front of him. "Do you have to dress like that?"

Stewart held out his arms and turned to the side. "What's wrong with the way I dress?"

"In case you haven't noticed, nobody in this town wears suits," said Murphy. "Damn few men even wear suits to church on Sunday, and they sure as hell don't wear green suits."

Stewart smiled. "You're just jealous."

"Jealous! You think I'm jealous? You're a part of the only black family in this town. Don't you think you should try to blend?"

"Blend? You want me to blend? I could start wearing bib overalls, suck on a straw, and have my teeth pulled. That would be blending, but I would still be a black man in a hick town. Besides, I think you're just jealous."

Murphy set his empty coffee cup on the table and started across the room. "Let's go visit Mr. Watson," he said opening the door. "I want to see if the man is innocent or guilty."

"Oh, you can tell just by talking with him, is that what I'm led to believe?" he asked following behind.

"That's my job," said Murphy getting into the sports car parked in front of his house. "Innocence or guilt. Besides, what did you mean I'm jealous of you? That will be the day when I'm jealous of an ugly black guy who wears clown suits."

"Clown suits!" he shouted as he got behind the wheel. "Why you white dumb ass ambulance chaser! I should make you walk to the jail. Besides, they'll probably keep you when we get there."

Murphy pointed ahead. "Let's just go," he said with a scowl.

◆◆◆

On the other side of town, a young woman opened the front door of the Sheriff's office and stepped inside. An older, stocky man in uniform was leaning over his desk leafing through a pile of paperwork.

She walked across the room and stopped just in front of his desk. "I wonder if I could see my husband?" she asked softly.

Sheriff Miller took a moment to finish reading and then looked up. "Are you Mrs. Watson?" he asked.

"I am," she replied. "I just want to see him for a few minutes."

"Do you plan on breaking him out?"

Kara paused her mouth open wide. "No, I don't," she stammered.

The big man picked the keys from his desk and handed them to her. "Here, just remember no one has ever escaped from my jail."

She took the keys from the man and started for the backroom. She opened the door and found a small room with just two jail cells. John was asleep on a small cot in the cell next to the door.

"John," she called out as she closed the door behind her.

The young man sprung to his feet. "Oh, it's you Kara," he said rubbing his eyes. "Am I ever glad to see you."

She thrust one of the keys in the door, turned it, and it swung open. "Are you alright?" she asked.

"I'm fine," he replied. "He let you have the keys to the place?"

She sat down on the edge of the cot. "He said no one has ever escaped from his jail. I don't know what that means." She leaned back on the cot. "So, when can you come home, John? I miss you already."

John got to his feet and walked across the room. "I'm not coming home, I guess," he said thrusting his hands in his pockets. "I'm in here for murder, and they don't let murderers out on bail or for any other reason."

"I thought you said that Harlan was okay when you left him last night," she said.

"He was okay," said John beginning to pace the floor. "At least, he was moving and making a groaning noise. I swear to God he was alive when I left him."

"Maybe, you hurt him bad enough he died after you left."

"He wasn't hurt that bad, Kara," he said. "He was cut up a little a few bruises but nothing bad." John returned to the cot and sat down on the edge. He held his head in his hands. "My God, Kara," he said softly. "What kind of a mess have I got myself into this time. I swear to God I regret the day we ever decided to move into this town."

Kara began to straighten his hair with her fingers. "I wish there was something I could do," she said.

John stared at the wall ahead his eyes fixed on the bars in the window. "When I was a kid my grandpa lived in a small shack at the edge of town. It was a small building only one room under a tar paper roof. Since it had never been painted and was exposed to the weather the boards were rotting near the ground. It had no electricity and it had no heat, and in the winter the wind howled through the cracks in the walls. With all that, he never complained. My grandpa would nearly freeze to death in that run-down shack, and yet he would worry about the neighbors who lived next door and whether or not they would have enough money for Christmas presents for their kids.

The company that Grandpa worked for all his life went out of business, and he lost his pension. The only money he had coming in was his social security checks, and he would sometimes give that away if he met someone who couldn't feed their kids.

To earn extra money, Grandpa would from time-to-time sell produce. He'd have a basket full of tomatoes, corn, and green beans that he would carry and go from door-to-door.

I'd go with him as he walked through the neighborhoods, and I would notice that after a while, he would be limping badly. I looked down at his feet and noticed that the soles of his shoes were all but missing. He was walking all over town on his bare feet.

I remember one day we were out selling produce and Grandpa stepped on a rock. The pain must have been unbearable. By the time we got to his place, he was bent over and hobbling on his sore feet. We got to the front of his house, and there on the porch was a bag of clothes that someone had left for him. Sitting beside the bag was a slightly used pair of work shoes.

"Isn't this wonderful?" he said searching through the bag and picking up the shoes. "You know what's even more wonderful?" he asked turning to me. "Just yesterday, I met some wonderful people who could use this stuff." John wiped a tear from his eye. "I never forgot that day, and I'll never forget that man. I guess when you think you've got it bad; there's always a bright side to everything. It's just I can't seem to find that bright side right now."

Just then, the door opened. "Mr. Watson?" said one of the two men as they entered the jail cell.

"Yeah," said John looking up.

"My name is Murphy Collins," he said offering his hand. "This is my friend, Stewart. "I'm your new court-appointed lawyer. May I sit down?" The two people scooted over on the small cot. Stewart leaned against the wall while Murphy sat on the edge of the cot.

John put his arm around his wife. "By the way, this is my wife, Kara."

"Nice to meet you," said Murphy giving her a quick glance. "John is there any chance we could have some privacy."

"Anything you have to say to me you can say in front of my wife," he said abruptly.

"Did you kill Harlan Steelman?" asked Murphy.

John jumped to his feet. "What did you say?"

"Did you kill Harlan Steeman?"

"No, I didn't kill him. What kind of question is that?"

Murphy opened his briefcase and pulled out a notepad. "Seemed like a fair question to me," said Murphy scribbling some notes. "You're in jail for murder, and I'm not." John stared at the man trying to decide what to say next. "Now that we got that out of the way, why don't you sit down and we'll try to figure out a way to convince twelve other people that you didn't do it." John didn't move. "Will you please sit down. It makes me nervous to have a murderer standing over me."

John stared at the man with a puzzled look and then smiled. "You don't look old enough to drive," he said taking a seat. "Are you sure you've got a lawyer's license or whatever you guys have to get."

Murphy leaned over and reached for his wallet in his back pocket. "I've got a lawyer's license and a driver's license. Wanna see 'em?"

John ignored the sarcastic question. "Have you ever tried a murder case?"

Murphy began writing on his notepad. "Nope. Never have."

"Ever helped with one?"

"Haven't even seen one."

"What makes you think you can help me then?"

Murphy stopped writing. "Ain't no difference between defending a chicken stealer and a murderer. The law works the same. Besides, what choice do you have? Unless you can afford your own lawyer, I think you're stuck with me."

Silence fell. John glanced at the floor and then at Murphy. "So, where do we go from here?"

"I have a few questions for you," said Murphy. "First off, let me ask you this. If you didn't kill Harlan, who did? I'm sure you have some idea."

"I don't know," he said. "I really don't know. All I know is that he was alive when I left."

"Which brings me to my second question: What happened last night? Why were you even over at his house?"

"He tried to rape my wife," John said. "And it wasn't the first time that's happened. Harlan Steelman has been a pain in my ass for a long time. This last thing with Kara was the last straw. I went over to his place to have it out with him. We fought, and I walked away. That's about the size of it."

"And he was alive when you left."

"He most certainly was," John said. "There's no way he died from the beating I gave him. There's no way at all."

"How can you say that?"

"I didn't hit him that hard," said John. "He was on the ground. I'll grant you that, but he was alright."

"What did he look like?"

"What do you mean?"

"Did he have any cuts? Was he bleeding?"

John glanced away. "Yeah, he was bloody. In fact, his head was covered in blood."

Murphy got to his feet and leaned over sticking a finger in John's face. "When you left him, he was lying on the ground, and his head was bathed in blood from the blows he took from you, hardly moving, and only able to make a groaning sound, and you want to tell me that he was okay?"

John jumped to his feet. "Hey, whose side are you on, anyhow?"

Murphy sat back down. "I'm just giving you a little taste of what's going to happen in court, now sit down." John didn't move. "I said sit your ass back down, John. I'm on your side. Besides, I don't want to piss you off. I know what an ass thumpin' you can give." John eased himself onto the cot. Murphy turned to Stewart. "I don't feel much love in this room. I don't think a group hug is going to happen."

"What else do you want to know?" asked John.

"Was there anyone else there? Did anyone witness the fight?"

"No, not a soul."

Murphy scribbled in his notebook. "You mentioned that you've had run-ins with Harlan in the past, so tell me about them."

John looked away. "There's not much to tell," he muttered.

Murphy put his pen down on his notebook. "Don't jerk me around," he said. "I need to know everything. I don't want to go into that courtroom and get blind-sighted. Do you understand?"

"Yes, I understand."

"Good. Now, tell me, what other confrontations have you had with Mr. Steelman," said Murphy picking up his pen.

"We squared off in the bar downtown."

Murphy began to write. "Did you exchange blows?"

"No."

"What happened?"

"Sheriff Miller broke it up."

Murphy stopped writing. "The Sheriff was a witness?"

John nodded his head.

Murphy turned to Stewart. "How do I get myself into these messes?" he asked and then turned back to John. "Was old man Steelman home at the time?"

John shook his head. "Didn't see him."

Murphy put his notebook away. "It's too bad," he said getting to his feet. "Someone did the town a favor by getting rid of Harlan Steeman, but, unfortunately, the law doesn't see it that way." He started for the door. "I'll keep in touch," he said and walked out the door.

A gust of wind sent waves of dust gliding across the massive front porch. Nolan Steelman settled into his favorite easy chair breathing a big sigh as he leaned back against the stained fabric. As always, it was dark in the room. Only spears of light filtered through a dirt encrusted window giving scant light to the room. He reached into his shirt pocket and removed a cigarette. He scratched a match on the bottom of his chair and touched the end of his cigarette bringing a bright orange glow to the darkness.

Tears trickled down both cheeks as he inhaled smoke deep into his lungs. It was a sweeter time all those years ago. The meadows were green, the corn high, and the rich countryside was forever bathed in warm sunshine. Young Harlan ran through the rows of corn his arms outstretched breaking stalks as he went.

A young man in bib overalls brought his tractor to a stop as he stared across the green field. "Harlan Steelman!" he screamed. Stillness fell on the field of corn. "Harlan, you come here! Right now!" "Still nothing. "Harlan, you've got ten seconds to get your butt up here!"

Slowly, the corn began to move. "Here I am, Pop," said the young boy as he appeared from the field. He ran across the lawn and stopped in front of the towering man sitting atop the big green tractor.

Nolan swung his leg around and jumped to the ground. He stared down at the boy. "What have I told you about running through the cornfield?" he asked leaning over with his hands on his knees.

The young boy leaned his head back to see his father's face. "I shouldn't do it?"

"I think you know the answer to that question."

Harlan bowed his head. "I'm sorry, Pop," he muttered. "I promise not to do it again."

Smoke rose gently from Nolan's lit cigarette disappearing into the darkness. Ash fell and landed on his lap. "All the years ago," he muttered aloud his eyes staring blankly into the dark. He snubbed out the last of his cigarette and dropped his hands into his lap. "Go wash up for dinner young man," he said aloud pointing into the darkness. He held out his hand for several moments and then gently cradled his head as he began to weep.

"God help me, I miss my boy already," he said aloud. The old man removed his handkerchief from his pocket and wiped his eyes. He took a deep breath and leaned back in his chair.

It was a long ago summer, the kind of summer from which dreams are made. Harlan bounced down the stairs and exploded through the front screen door. He was just sixteen and was dressed up for his first date.

"Where are you going, son?" asked his father.

Harlan turned to find his dad sitting on the front porch swing. "I'm taking a girl to the dance tonight, Pop," he said with a smile. "This is my first date, and I'm really nervous."

"Come over here and sit down, son," said Nolan moving to one side.

"But I'm already late," said the young boy.

"This will only take a minute."

Harlan jumped on the swing and started it in motion. "What do you want, Pop?" he asked.

"I just wanted to talk to you for a minute about girls."

"Oh, I already know about that stuff."

"What stuff?"

"The birds and bees and that kind of stuff."

Nolan smiled. "That's not what I wanted to talk to you about," he said. "I'm sure you've learned enough about that from your friends. No, that's not what I wanted to talk to you about although I probably should warn you of the dangers of having sex. What I wanted to talk with you about is girls and the respect they deserve." Nolan turned in time to see his son as he rolled his eyes. "I know you think it's corny, but I'm just telling you, son that you must treat all girls with respect. They deserve it."

"Why, Pop? What's so special about girls?"

"Let me ask you something. Would you spit on your mother?"

Harlan paused. He looked into his father's eyes to see if this was a trick question. "Of course not," he replied.

"Of course you wouldn't," he said placing a hand on Harlan's shoulder. "You have too much respect for her. Son, I want you to remember one thing. Sex with a woman is a grand thing. I'm not denying it, but it only lasts for a few minutes. What's really important is the sweet and tender love of a woman. If you can get a woman to give you that, you'll know true happiness, and the only way you'll get it is to show her respect. Do you understand what I'm trying to tell you, son?"

Harlan stared blankly at his father. "So, what you're saying is I shouldn't spit on my date."

Nolan paused and then began to laugh. "Go on with you," he said pushing his son out of the swing. "Have a good time and get back here early."

The old man touched a lighted match to a cigarette and breathed in deeply. He pulled a handkerchief from his pocket and brushed away the tears from his face. "God, those were good times all those years ago," he muttered staring at the floor.

Suddenly, there was a knocking on the front door. "Come in," the old man called out.

Two men eased open the door and stepped inside. "Mr. Steelman, my name is Murphy Collins, and this is my associate, Stewart Hatfield."

Nolan snubbed out his cigarette. "Sit down over there," he said pointing at the couch.

The two men walked across the dark room and stood in front of a tattered corduroy sofa. A large brown and white cat was curled in a ball in the center of the couch. Murphy stared at the animal and turned to the old man. "You got a cat crapped out on the sofa."

"Knock him off."

"What?"

"Just knock him off the sofa," said Nolan. "He knows he don't belong up there."

Murphy stared at the animal. He turned to Stewart. "You do it," he said. "You're better with animals."

Stewart turned to his friend. "Was that an ethnic slur?"

"What do you mean?"

"You know, my background and such. The jungles of Africa and that kind of shit."

"They got housecats in the jungles of Africa?"

Nolan cleared his throat. "Hey, Dumbass!" he shouted. The animal lifted his head. "Get the hell out of here!" Before he finished his command, the cat in one fluid motion got to his feet and darted out the door.

Murphy shifted the stack of papers he was carrying, and they slipped from his hands scattering on the floor. "Shit," he muttered and bent down to collect his papers.

"Christ," muttered Stewart bending down. "Why the hell don't you get yourself a briefcase?"

"Yeah, why don't ya?" asked Nolan lighting another cigarette.

Murphy scowled. He scooped up the remainder of the papers and got to his feet. "Mr. Steelman, I represent John Watson and would like to ask you some questions if you don't mind."

The old man stiffened. "You're probably the last person in the world I want to see right now."

"I know, sir," said Murphy. "I apologize for this intrusion. Wouldn't blame you if you asked me to leave, but please understand that I'm just doing my job."

Nolan paused as he thought about it. "You sure got your nerve," he said with a frown. Murphy remained silent. "Alright, but make it quick. Somehow the idea of helping the lawyer of the man who killed my son doesn't set too well with me."

"Okay, Mr. Steelman, we'll keep it to just a few questions," he said. "Now, as I understand it, John came over here last night to see your son. Would you mind telling me where you were at the time?"

"I was in Chicago," said Nolan. "Had to sign some papers on my brother's estate. He died last year and left everything to me." The old man dropped his head. "After last night, I guess I'm the only kin left."

"Tell me, Mr. Steelman, how long were you gone?"

"Just long enough to sign the damn papers. Got home here about seven this morning maybe later."

"What do you mean maybe later?"

"Well, I'm not sure of the time what with the shock of seeing my boy lying there and all."

"How did you get there? Did you drive?"

"Chartered a plane over in Springfield."

"Mr. Steelman, I hate to ask you this, but could you describe what you saw when you walked through the door?"

Nolan took a deep breath and got to his feet. He grimaced as he stared across the room. "You know I just did this for the police."

"I know Mr. Steeman, and I'm really sorry about this, but I really need to hear this from you."

The old man ran his hand through his hair and walked to the other side of the room. Murphy and Stewart followed him and stopped at one corner of the room. The floor was soaked in dried blood. Spatters of dark red covered the walls and furniture. Nolan's voice began to shake. "He was lying face-up right there," he said pointing at the floor. It was horrible, just horrible," he said turning away. I've never seen so much blood. I could hardly recognize him."

"I'm sorry, Mr. Steelman, but did you say he was face-up?"

Nolan turned and stared at the floor as if remembering the scene. "Yes, I'm sure of it. He was face-up." The old man began to weave uncontrollably as if he were about to fall. "I still can't believe it," he muttered holding out his hands as if to give himself balance.

Stewart grabbed a folding chair and rushed across the floor. "Sit down, Mr. Steelman," he said softly.

Nolan eased himself into the chair and bowed his head. "I'm so sorry," he muttered as he began to weep.

"We'll be going now, Mr. Steelman," said Stewart. "We've bothered you enough for one day."

Murphy said nothing. He stared intently at the crime scene. He squatted down and lowered his head until it was in line with the blood spatters on the wall. "Interesting," he muttered. "Very interesting."

Stewart laid his hand on his friend's shoulder. "Come on, Murph," he said. "Let's leave the kind man alone now."

Murphy got to his feet. He scooped up his papers and started for the door. "Thank you so much, Mr. Steelman," he said pushing open the front door. "You've been a big help."

The old man turned to the two men. "Hey!" he shouted. "Give your client a message for me, will you?" Murphy stopped and turned. "Tell him if the state don't get him, I will."

The two men glanced at each other and left the room.

The next morning brought warm sunshine spreading over the small town. Melvin turned his car down a neighborhood street and stopped in front of an older house. A young man ran out the front door and across the lawn.

"What's up?" Travis asked opening the car door.

"Get in," said Melvin. "We need to go to my house and talk with Lone Wolf. He's been acting a little strange lately."

"What's the matter with him?"

"I'm not quite sure. All I know is he's been awfully quiet. I think it might have something to do with Sara. I heard him say her name."

"What do you mean he said her name? What's he been talking about?"

"I don't know," said Melvin turning down another street. "He's been sitting on the floor kind of cross-legged and just muttering out loud. It's been really freaky. I say stuff to him, but it's kind of like he doesn't hear me. That's when I decided to come and get you. Maybe, you might know what to do."

Travis smiled. "You're scared of him, aren't you?"

Melvin turned to his friend. "No, I'm not."

"Yes, you are."

"No, I'm not."

"You are."

"Am not!" Jesus, that's the last time I'll ask help from you."

"Well, what do you want me to do?"

"Just talk with him," said Melvin. "He seems to understand you like one beast communicating with another."

Travis glanced at his friend and then turned back to the road ahead. "Speaking of Sara, have you heard anything about her?"

"Just that she's still unconscious," he said. "They don't want to call it a coma yet. I guess that sounds worse than unconscious."

"We have to get into that hospital to see her."

"No problem," said Melvin. "We'll go right after we check on Lone Wolf."

"You make it sound so easy. They aren't going to let us in."

"Why not?"

"We're too young and besides, they don't let anyone in for someone in that serious of a condition."

"Don't worry, we'll get in," said Melvin as he turned into his own driveway. He stopped the car, and the two boys got out. They walked across the lawn and up to the front door. "Right now, let's see how the Indian chief is doing," he said opening the front door.

"Lone Wolf!" cried Melvin. The two boys walked across the living room. "Where are you?" They stopped to listen for a reply. "He was right here on the floor when I left," he said pointing at a corner of the room. "Let's split up. You go that way, and I'll check over there."

Travis swept through the house searching each room as he went. "Find anything?" he asked as he returned to the living room.

"Not a thing," replied Melvin. "I think I know where he is though."

"Where is that?"

"I'll bet he's gone to the hospital to see Sara," said Melvin with a smile. "Let's go!"

◆◆◆

It was nearly the end of the work shift when Nurse Clara dropped a pile of papers on the reception desk. She was a heavyset black woman nearly six feet in height. "Thank God this day is almost over," she said leaning on the desk.

"Bad day?" asked the woman behind the desk.

"A day like none other. I swear every patient in this place had a problem today. I never seen nothing like it."

"Well, your day is almost over. Maybe, you can go home and soak your feet,"

"That do sound nice," said Clara standing upright. "I figure though if that husband of mine don't have dinner on I'll be soaking his head!"

"Let me ask you something," said the receptionist. "What about Sara in 301? Any change?"

"Not one bit," she whispered. "I don't think that poor girl is ever coming out of that state she's in." Clara leaned forward. "They can call it whatever they want, but to me that girl is in a coma. Poor little thing all curled up like that. Sure hope they catch that Indian that did this. Never did trust that man. Ain't right for a body to be running around in the woods like that. Just ain't civilized."

"You know, Clara, there are those who don't think he did it. I mean after all, why would he carry her all the way to the hospital. My God, that must have been three to four miles. Besides, it just don't make sense to let all those people see him if he had anything to hide."

Clara began to shake her head. "I don't care what they say, he done it. That's all there is to it. He's a savage running free, and he broke the law. He needs to be punished."

Suddenly, Clara jumped. She turned in the direction of the hallway. "Lands sakes, what was that?"

The woman behind the desk got to her feet. "What was what?"

Clara walked over to the hall and looked both ways. "I don't believe it. I must have been seeing things."

"What did you see?"

"It looked like the tail end of a dog. I know that sounds crazy, but that's what it looked like. It was just marching down the aisle as pretty as you please."

"Where did it go?"

"I have no idea. Besides, I may have been just seeing things. Maybe, it's time for me to go home," she said starting for the door.

"Good night, Clara. Take care."

"See you in the morning."

There was very little light in Room 301. The overhead light was turned off, and the curtains partially drawn. A young woman laid unconscious in a hospital bed. In spite of the fact that she hasn't moved since the accident, the side rails are up to avoid the possibility of her falling out of bed. She was laying on one side, her legs curled as if in a fetal position. Her hair has been pulled back revealing her soft ashen skin. Medical people come and go. They examine, probe, and diagnose, but nothing changes. Her body sometimes twitches, her eyes dart underneath their lids, but the young woman remains oblivious to the world around her.

"Well, how are we doing?" asked a woman in white as she entered the room. She unhooked the nearly empty IV and replaced it with a full one. "My, aren't you still the prettiest thing," she said smoothing the sheets in her bed. "I get so scared when I see still another young person in a comma. Yes, I said the C word. Lord knows I've seen enough in this place to know what a comma looks like."

The woman leaned over the bed and ran her fingers through the girl's silky hair. "Honey, if you're planning on coming back, you need to do it soon. That's just the way it is. If you stay this way too long, you simply can't come back. I've seen it too many times." She paused as she studied the young woman hoping for a reaction. She lightly patted her arm. "You take care, and I'll see you later on," she said and walked out of the room.

As a storm rolled in from the west, dark clouds tumbled across the sky hiding the sunlight from the earth below. Suddenly, a shadow appeared in the room. It moved effortlessly across the floor and disappeared into the darkness. A large man emerged from a corner of the room. He walked over to the window and closed the curtains. It was dark now in the room the only light was from the soft glow of a small nightlight near the bed.

The big man walked over to the side of the bed and stared down at the young woman. In spite of the dim lighting, he could see her small, frail body lying innocently in the bed and the almost serene look on her face that made her look as if she were about to awake from a night's sleep. He leaned a little closer. It didn't seem possible but there was even a slight hint of a smile.

Lone Wolf leaned back. He took a deep breath and let it out slowly. He had been trained for this when he was a young man. He had seen it performed once years ago but had never actually tried it himself. He took another deep breath. His hands shook as he leaned over the bed once again.

Slowly, he took the young woman's small head and cupped it between his massive hands. He applied a slight pressure and leaned his own head back to stare at the ceiling above. "Homay, Hocktah, Edah," he muttered softly still staring at the ceiling. Lone Wolf paused and glanced down at

Sara. He studied her face looking for a reaction. "Homay, Hocktah, Edah…Homay, Hocktah, Edah" He continued the chant for several more minutes and then stopped. He glanced down at the girl, still no reaction. He held her head even tighter and began to softly recite an ancient Indian prayer. It was a prayer that asked God to have mercy on those who had recently died. It also asked Him to grant a second chance to the young and the innocent.

Lone Wolf finished his prayer and slowly withdrew his hands from her face. He stared at the young woman searching for a sign of life. Minutes passed, and still nothing. "Come on, little girl," he muttered as he began to pace the floor. He walked across the room and checked the hallway. He returned to her bedside and stared down at the young woman.

Suddenly, she moved. It was a very slight movement of her right arm as she picked it straight up and let it drop. Lone Wolf leaned forward and studied her facial features. She was a pretty girl with long blond hair that fell in all directions.

Then it happened. There was a slight twitch of her cheek, and then her eyes opened wide. Lone Wolf smiled as he moved back. She blinked her eyes several times and then opened and closed her mouth.

"Sara," he called out softly. "Can you hear me?"

She grunted and smacked her lips together several times.

"How do you feel?" he asked.

She blinked her eyes trying to focus her vision and then slowly turned in the bed until she was on her back. She quickly glanced around the room and then focussed on the man standing by her bed. She studied his face as if trying to recall his identity. "Lone Wolf?" she questioned.

The big man smiled. "Yes, it's me," he said softly. "How do you feel?"

She glanced down at her body. "I guess I'm alright. Where am I?"

"You're in the hospital."

"What happened?"

"You had nasty fall, hit head. You be ok now."

Approaching footsteps resounded down the hall. Two young men stopped in the doorway. "I knew we'd find him here," said Melvin. "What are you doing here?"

Lone Wolf stepped back to reveal the young woman lying awake in her bed.

"Oh, my God!" Travis exclaimed as he stepped forward. "She's awake." They stopped at the side of her bed. "How are you?"

"I'm fine," she said softly. She turned back to Lone Wolf. "You did this, didn't you? You brought me out of my sleep. I don't know how I know, but I do." She reached out and took his massive hand in hers. "Thank you, Lone Wolf."

The big man smiled. "You be fine now."

Travis leaned over the bed. "I hate to ask you these questions right now, but it's important. Do you think you can try to remember for us?"

Sara rubbed her face. "I'll try," she said. "What do you want to know?"

"You fell and hit your head. You've been unconscious since then. Can you remember what you were doing?"

"I don't know," she muttered staring past him. "It seems like such a long time ago."

"I know, Sara, and I'm so sorry to do this to you, but we need to know what happened that night. You see, Lone Wolf carried you all the way into town to the hospital, and now the Sheriff thinks he is responsible for your injuries."

"What?"

"They think Lone Wolf attacked you. That's why it's so important for you to remember."

Sara turned and stared into the darkness. "He was chasing me," she said coldly. "I remember that."

"Who was chasing you?" asked Travis.

"I'm not sure," she muttered. "I couldn't see him. It was so dark that night. I just remember running and running. I got inside my house and I thought I'd be safe there, but he broke in. God, I was so scared."

"Sara, think hard," said Travis. "Did you see his face?"

The young woman became silent. She stared into the darkness. "I remember the house was dark. I don't know why. It's usually always lit up. I remember turning on a light in the kitchen and looking down to see…oh, now I remember who it was that night."

"Who was it?"

"Harlan…Harlan Steelman, that's who it was."

"Are you sure?"

"I'm positive," she said sitting up in bed. "Sorry, Melvin, I know he's your kin."

"He was my kin," said Melvin.

"Why? What do you mean by that?"

"Oh, that's right," said Melvin. "You don't know. Of course, how could you know?" He glanced at Travis. "Harlan is dead."

"Oh, my God!" said Sara. "What happened?"

"We don't really know," said Travis. "But Dad is in jail accused of murdering him."

"I don't believe it!" she shouted. She paused and searched the room. "Where's Lone Wolf? He was here just a minute ago."

The two boys searched the room and then started for the door. "We've got to be going, Sara," said Travis. "I'm so glad you're feeling better."

"Will you come back to see me?" she asked.

"I promise I will," he replied standing in the doorway.

"I love you," she said softly.

Travis turned. He stared at the girl sitting up in bed. "Huh?" he said.

"I said I love you."

Travis's mouth dropped open. "Wow!" he said and walked out of the room.

CHAPTER 9

The summer seemed to rush by, and already it was the hot, sultry days of August. It was the eve of the murder trial of John Watson, and the town was abuzz with gossip. The last big trial had been two years ago, and involved Fred Strange accused by his neighbor of running over his cat with a lawnmower. Fred was acquitted for lack of evidence. The judge said he needed more than a mangled dead cat. Since then, there have only been small trials involving shoplifting, noise violations, and one case of jaywalking.

A young woman opened the jail cell door and walked inside. "Hi, John," she said taking a seat on a small wooden chair. "How are you?"

The young man had been asleep on the small cot against the far wall. "I'm fine," he said swinging his legs around and sitting on the edge of the bed. "It's so late. What are you doing here?"

"I know it's late, and I'm sorry to bother you," she said staring at the floor. "It's just that...I just needed to talk with you. I wouldn't have come if I had thought you'd be asleep."

"Seems like that's all I ever do anymore," he said rubbing his eyes. "Not much to do in here as you can see. What's on your mind?"

Kara picked at a loose nail in the floor with the side of her shoe. "I just wanted to say I'm sorry," she said softly.

John stopped rubbing his face. He looked up. "Sorry for what?" he asked.

Kara took a deep breath. "I'm sorry for everything," she said. "I'm sorry for your getting in trouble, for the way our lives have turned out, and especially for the way I've acted."

John frowned. "What do you mean the way you acted?"

"Come on, John, you have to admit I haven't been the best wife to you lately," she said. "I'm even surprised you've put up with me since we moved to this town."

"You've been under a lot of stress, Kara," he said. "I'm really surprised you've stayed with me what with all the things that have happened to us."

Kara looked up at the man sitting on the bed. "All I can say is I'm sorry for the way I acted, and I'll try to do better."

John rubbed the back of his neck. "Kara, is it possible it was because of him?"

"Because of who?"

Harlan Steelman."

"What about Harlan Steelman?"

"Is it possible you were still in love with Harlan?"

Kara paused and looked away. "It's not that," she said glancing his way. "I never really was in love with Harlan even when we were kids. That I'm sure of."

"Then, what is it? What was Harlan Steelman to you?"

"It's funny," she said with a far off smile. "I've often wondered that myself. It's almost as if he had a spell on me. I remember when we were kids I wanted to be with him, and yet I never thought of him as handsome and he certainly wasn't kind. Hell, I remember when we were kids he stole my lunch on the way to school one day. When I said something to him, he punched me in the eye. Can you believe it? I had a black eye thanks to that guy."

John cleared his throat. "Can I ask you a question? That time all those years ago when you were attacked, you always contended that you never knew who did it. I always wondered if you were just protecting Harlan. Did you really lose your memory?"

Kara frowned. "I was knocked out, John," she barked. "I really don't have any idea who did it."

John looked away. "Well, I guess we'll never know for sure now that he's dead, but there's no doubt in my mind that he did it."

Kara got to her feet and walked across the small room. She sat down next to her husband and took his hand in hers. "It was a long time ago, John. You've got to let it go. He's dead now, so there's nothing we can do about it now. Besides, we have more important things to worry about right now."

John turned and looked at his wife. "Yes, I suppose you're right," he said. He began to smile. "It feels good having you with me. For the first time, I feel like it's going to be okay. I can't explain it, but somehow I think we're going to make it."

Kara looked up at her husband. Her eyes sparkled as she smiled. She gripped his hands firmly with both of hers. "I know we're going to make it, John. I just know it."

◆◆◆

The next morning brought the promise of another hot August day. The trial was set for nine o'clock in the morning, and by eight o'clock nearly everyone in town was on the front steps of the courthouse hoping to get a seat inside.

It was an old building dating back to the turn of the century. With its three stories and ornate design, it was the most impressive building in the county. Inside, a young man was escorted to a place at the front of the room. The room became quiet as all eyes watched John Watson take his seat. Nearly a hundred people were crammed into the back of the room many left standing for the lack of seating.

Sitting at a table across the aisle was Harrison Bentley, the County Prosecutor. Harrison had held the position of County Prosecutor for so many years no one could remember who had proceeded him. He was a distinguished looking man of near seventy years of age with snow-white hair and a statuesque physique that still turned heads.

John glanced at the clock on the wall. It was after nine o'clock, and his attorney was still not there. He looked across the aisle at Harrison. He was smiling. It was a smile of victory because he knew that the first points of this legal match had gone in his favor. Judge Hatfield had no tolerance for tardiness, and it was well past nine o'clock.

The Judge entered the room. He was an older man of African descent. His hair was a silver-gray that from a distance seemed to glow. He stopped and stared at the back of the courtroom. "Bailiff, get those people whom are standing in the back there out of my courtroom," he said taking a seat behind his oak desk. "You know better than that. There's only so many chairs in this courtroom, and that's all the spectators I'll allow." He paused and then turned to the clerk. "Willard, where the hell is Murphy? Isn't he representing the defendant in this case?"

Before he could answer, the courtroom doors opened and in marched two young men. "Sorry, your honor," said Murphy dropping a pile of paper on the desk. "I got hung up in traffic."

Judge Hatfield leaned forward. "Traffic!" he shouted. "Traffic in this town! Who the hell do you think you're talking to?"

"I'm sorry your honor. I won't let it happen again."

"You're damn right you won't, Murph. Now, I've warned you about this before. Don't screw with me this time. I'm at the end of my rope with you."

"I promise, your Honor," said Murphy shuffling through his stack of paperwork. "It won't happen again."

The Judge leaned back in his chair. "Good! Now, sit down," he said. "Alright, let's get this show on the road. Mr.

Bentley, do you wish to make an opening statement to the jury?"

"Yes, I do, your Honor," he said getting to his feet. He slowly walked across the room and stood in front of the seated jurors. "Ladies and gentlemen of the jury, the prosecution will prove that John Watson did willfully and with forethought murder Harlan Steelman, a respected leader in our community. The bad blood between these two men was no secret. I have witnesses who will testify that they saw these two men involved in confrontations, and I even have Sheriff Miller who will testify under oath that he heard the defendant threaten to kill the deceased."

He walked to the center of the courtroom and turned to face the jury. "You know you twelve people are very fortunate," he said with a smile. "Many trials can be very tricky. Sometimes the facts are overwhelming, and the truth is not always that easy to see. What we have here today is a trial that will be over with in no time, and you will be back home bragging to your friends and neighbors about how easy it was. Because what we have here is a clear case of murder. The defendant, John Watson, did willfully commit the brutal and murderous act by storming over to Harlan Steelman's house and beating him with his fists until he was dead."

The Prosecutor walked back to the wooden railing in front of the jury. "In keeping with the theme of this trial, I'm going to spare you the exasperation of a long speech. In fact, I'm going to go sit down and turn the floor over to my colleague, Mr. Collins."

Murphy got to his feet. He smiled as he looked at each one of the jurors. "My colleague is right you know," he said walking slowly across the room. This trial really shouldn't take long. In fact, we shouldn't even be here in the first place. You will soon see that there is not enough evidence to convict my client, and in fact I'm surprised there was enough for a grand jury to even bound him over for trial."

Murphy put both hands on the railing and leaned forward. "Mr. Bentley has had plenty of time to prepare his case against John Watson, but the best he could come up with is flimsy testimony from people who saw my client at odds with the deceased and some have even heard him threaten Harlan Steelman, but no one can truthfully say they ever saw John Watson even so much as lay a finger on Harlan Steelman."

Murphy walked to the center of the courtroom and turned to the jury. "So, why are we here? That's a very good question. Perhaps, it's because we needed someone to blame, and John seemed the most likely. That could be it. Hope it's not. Hardly seems right to try a man for no more reason than that. But I guess that's what we're here for, and that's to find the truth and what is really right. I think you'll soon discover the truth, and the truth is that John Watson did not kill Harlan Steelman. You'll acquit him, and we'll all go home where we belong. Thank you, ladies and gentlemen of the jury."

Murphy returned to his seat. Low murmurs swept over the courtroom.

Judge Hatfield lightly tapped his gavel on his desktop. "I want it quiet in here," he said loudly across the room. He turned to the Prosecution. "Mr. Bentley, are you ready to present your case?"

"I am, your Honor," he said shuffling through a stack of papers. "The Prosecution calls Sheriff Miller to the stand."

The bailiff stepped outside the courtroom and returned with the Sheriff. He escorted him to the front of the room and swore him to tell the truth.

Harrison got to his feet. "Sheriff Miller, you've represented the law in this town for over thirty years. Isn't that correct?"

"Thirty-two, to be exact," he said taking the witness chair.

"So, it's safe to say that you're an experienced lawman who has seen just about everything."

"I guess you could say that."

"In your experience as a lawman how would you characterize the relationship between Harlan Steelman and the defendant, John Watson?"

The Sheriff turned to the jury. "In my experience I'd say there was bad blood between those two. I had a feeling something bad was going to happen."

"What do you think was the reason for this bad blood as you called it?"

"Hell, those two had been fighting over the same woman since they was kids," he said with a smile. "Course, I'm real sure they ain't the first two men to fight over some dame." Nervous smiles appeared across the courtroom.

"So, these two have been at odds since they were kids. Is that right?"

"Sure is."

"Did you ever see them in a fight?"

The Sheriff glanced at the ceiling. "Can't say as I have," he muttered. "I'd bet the farm that they've been in some kind of scrape though, but can't remember ever actually seeing them fighting. I did see them square off though."

"Square off. What do you mean by that?"

"Seen 'em in Coonies one day circling each other like roosters. I broke it up before it ever got started, but they were headed for a fight then."

Harrison walked up to the witness chair. "Now, Sheriff Miller, did you happen to hear any threats made during that particular incident?"

The Sheriff turned to the jury. "Sure did," he said pointing at John. "I heard the defendant over there tell Harlan he was going to kill him."

"I'm sorry, Sheriff Miller. Could you repeat that one more time for us?"

"I said he told Harlan Steelman that he was going to kill him."

"Thank you, Sheriff Miller," said Harrison turning to the defendant's table. "Your witness."

John leaned towards Murphy. "It really didn't happen…"

"Sheriff Miller, you're a married man, aren't you?" asked Murphy getting to his feet.

The big man leaned back in chair. "Thirty years this December."

"You must love your wife very much."

The Sheriff glanced at the judge. "Sure do, but I don't see what this has to do with anything."

"In spite of all that, you must certainly have arguments with her, don't you?"

"Well, yeah. We've had a few spats, I guess."

"Ever have a time when you're right, she's wrong, and she won't agree with you?"

"I suppose so."

"Isn't that frustrating, Sheriff?" asked Murphy walking over to the witness stand. "Doesn't it make you mad?"

"I guess so."

"Did you ever get so mad that you called her a name or cursed at her."

"Yeah, I can remember a time when…"

"Did you ever threaten her? Did you ever tell her you were going to hit her or maybe you're really mad and you tell her you're going to kill her? You don't mean it, but it just came out seeing as how you were so angry."

"I don't think so," he said crossing his arms. "I wouldn't ever tell my wife I was going to kill her."

"Oh, I don't think you would either, but we all say things in anger we regret later, don't you agree?"

"Yeah, but I would never tell my wife I was going to kill her."

"Now think, Sheriff," said Murphy. "In all the thirty years you've been married you've never once been so darn mad at her that you said you were going to kill her?"

Miller paused. He glanced at the judge. "Can't say as I have."

"Oh, come on now, Sheriff," said Murphy walking away. "You don't want me to bring Mrs. Miller up here to see if she has a better memory than you, do you? Now, tell me, isn't it just possible that even once in all those thirty years you might have uttered those words?"

Miller looked at Murphy. He sneered as if cornered in a trap. "Yeah, I suppose so."

"You suppose what?"

"I suppose I could have said that I was going to kill her."

"Thank you, Sheriff Miller," said Murphy returning to his seat. "You're excused."

John leaned towards Murphy. "I don't know much about it, but it looks to me like we did good on that one."

Murphy smiled. "Ya, I'd say we scored one for the home team."

"Your Honor, the Prosecution calls Dr. Higgins to the stand," said Harrison standing at his desk.

John leaned over to Murphy. "Nice to see Willard sober," he whispered.

"Doc Higgins has a drinking problem?" asked Murphy.

"Where the hell have you been?" he asked. "I heard about that the first day I came back to town."

"Doctor Higgins, you have been the County Coroner for a good many years. Is that right?"

"Next year will make forty," he replied.

"Tell me something, Doctor, were you called out to examine Harlan Steelman's body?"

"I was."

"And what was your determination?"

"From what I could see, someone had beaten the crap out of Harlan," he said with a smile.

"So, I can safely say that someone beat him in the face until he was dead."

"That's pretty much what I said."

"His head didn't hit an object such as a stair step or a chair when he fell to the floor, did it?"

"Wasn't anything around for him to hit," said the doctor.

"So Doctor Higgins, in your experience, what was the cause of death?"

He turned to the jury. "Harlan Steelman died from a massive trauma to the head, and from the nature of the wounds, I would say that it was caused by blows from someone's fists."

"Thank you, Doctor," said Harrison returning to his seat. "Your witness, Mr. Collins."

Murphy got to his feet. "Now, Doctor Higgins, You told the court that you've been County Coroner for nearly forty years. Is that right?"

The old man shifted his weight. "That's right."

Murphy leaned casually on the railing just in front of the witness stand. "Over the course of all those years, you've seen quite a lot things, haven't you?"

"I don't know. What do you mean by things?"

"You know, things in the world of death. After forty years of dealing with all forms of death you've just about seen them all, haven't you?"

Higgins smiled. "Yeah, I suppose you're right. Not much to be proud of, but, yes, I guess I've seen about as much as the next man."

"Yes, I suppose you have," said Murphy with a broad smile. "I guess something like this case is kind of rare, isn't it Doctor?"

"How do you mean?"

"You know, someone getting murdered," said Murphy. "I got to believe that most of the deaths in a back woods area like this are either accidental or simply a natural death. Is that about the size of it?"

"Oh, by all means," he said rubbing the back of his neck. "The last time we had something like this was when Otis Barns was shot in the head by his wife, Gladys, and hell that was probably ten or twelve years ago."

"So, what you're saying, Doctor, is that you have forty years of experience as a coroner but very limited experience when it comes to investigating a murder, is that about the sum of it?"

The old man leaned back and gently laid his hands on his protruding stomach. "Yes, I suppose that's correct. Of course, that doesn't mean that I am unable to perform my job."

"In your testimony earlier, you said that when you investigated the crime scene, you found that Harlan had been beaten with fists and had fallen to the floor. Is that correct?"

"Yes, that's right," said the doctor.

Murphy leaned over the railing. "Well then, Doctor Higgins, how do you explain the blood spatters on the wall next to where the body was found?"

Higgins sat up in his chair. "Blood spatters! I don't remember any blood spatters on any wall. There was a pool of blood on the floor and the body was covered in blood, but that was all there was!"

"Doctor Higgins, I was there that morning and saw it myself. It looked like someone had hit Harlan in the head with a club of some kind to spray that much blood on the wall."

Higgins slowly eased back in his chair. His blank stare turned downwards. "I must have missed that," he said.

"You must have missed that. Is that what you said? We're all wondering what else you missed. You see, Doctor Higgins, this is not a small point that you missed. It quite possibly changes the entire scenario of how Harlan died. It appears he was hit in the head with a blunt instrument after he was down on the floor. Was there a search for such an instrument?"

"No, sir," replied Higgins.

Murphy slowly walked to the center of the courtroom. "Now, Doctor Higgins, I understand you were on vacation at the time they called you about Harlan's death. In fact, they tell me you were on a boat out on Clear Fork Lake with your line in the water. Did you catch anything?"

Higgins smiled. "No, afraid I didn't."

"Well, that's a shame, Doctor," said Murphy. "It's an even bigger shame that you had to come off your vacation even if it was for a day."

"Oh, I didn't mind," he said. "It comes with the job."

"Yes, I suppose it does," said Murphy. "That's too bad you didn't catch anything though, but hell the fun is in trying, isn't it Doc? Nothing better than sitting in a boat on a warm day just you and old Jack."

"Jack?"

"You know… Jack Daniel's."

Higgins smiled. "Well, as a matter of fact, old Jack Daniel's was there with me that day."

"Well, that's what vacations are for, aren't they, Doc? Ain't no sin to have a few belts on vacation. How many do you think you had on that morning?"

Higgins chuckled. "Hell, old Jack was half gone when I found out about Harlan."

Murphy walked quickly over to the witness stand and leaned towards Higgins. "So, it's safe to say that you performed the investigation of the death of Harlan Steelman after consuming half of a bottle of whiskey. Is that correct, Doctor Higgins?"

Higgin's face went blank.

Murphy returned to his seat. "That's all, Doctor Higgins. You may sit down."

John leaned over to Murphy. "I don't know much about this, but I'd say we just won another round."

"So far, so good," said Murphy. "We'll see how the rest of the week goes."

◆◆◆

The days sped by as more testimony was introduced. It was already Friday, and Murphy was sitting in the courtroom an hour before the trial was to resume. He was busy reviewing paperwork when the door to the courtroom opened, and in walked Kara Watson.

"I was told I would find you here," she said as she sat down next to him.

"Good morning, Kara," said Murphy. "What can I do for you?"

"No," she said. "It's what I can do for you." She handed him six leather bound books. He opened one of them and scanned through the pages. "Turn to page sixty-three," she said.

Murphy thumbed through the pages and began to read. He soon finished, closed the book, and laid it on the table.

"Where did you get this?" he asked.

"I was cleaning his bedroom and found them under his bed."

"We actually still have a search warrant, so this is not illegally obtained. Did he see you take it?"

"He wasn't even home."

"You know that as a wife of the defendant you don't have to testify, but I really need you to get on the stand. Are you okay with that?"

"Not a problem," she replied.

"Well, I just want you to know that the Prosecutor is going to be kind of rough," said Murphy. "He's been waiting for an opportunity like this."

Kara smiled. "I don't care. I just want to do something to help, so let's do it!" she said.

It was shortly after nine o'clock when the judge took his seat and the jurors filed into the courtroom. Judge Hatfield leaned over his desk. "Would counsel approach the bench?" he asked. The two men got to their feet and slowly walked to the front of the courtroom. "I don't mean to criticize, but this thing has been dragging on long enough. It's Friday already, and it just don't seem like we're making any progress. Do you understand what I mean here?"

Murphy leaned forward. "No, I'm afraid I don't. Are you saying I should eliminate some of my witnesses in the interest of saving time?"

The Judge pointed a finger at Murphy. "You know, it's that kind of attitude that makes me want to charge you with contempt of court!"

"I'm sorry your Honor," said Murphy. "I meant no disrespect. I simply…"

"Call your first witness," said the Judge leaning back in his chair.

"Your Honor, the defense calls Kara Watson to the stand."

Murphy glanced at the Prosecutor. He crossed his legs and smiled confidently.

"Now, Kara, you have agreed to go on the stand, have you not?"

"Yes, I have," she replied.

"I'm going to ask you some very, very personal questions, and I want you to know that I wouldn't do it if it wasn't important. Do you understand?"

"Yes, I understand."

Murphy walked closer to the stand. "When you were just a young girl, you had something happen to you that was very disturbing. Would you please tell the court in your words what happened?"

"I remember it was a warm summer evening, the kind of night when the crickets are loud and the breeze ever so soft. Harlan and I had been dating off and on. I wasn't quite sure if there was a future with him. I reckon I was more or less fooled by his fancy cars and all his money. We were sitting on his front porch when we got into an argument. As always, it was a fight about sex. I was old-fashion enough to want to wait until after marriage. He wanted it now. It got pretty bad that night. I remember taking off his class ring and throwing it at him and storming off into the night. I think I had made up my mind that night that I wanted to marry John.

Kara turned to the jury. "It was dark that night. I remember I could barely see the road as I started walking the quarter mile back to town. It was such a quiet night I can't believe I didn't hear him, but all of a sudden someone came up on me and hit me real hard. I hit the ground and must have skidded ten feet. It didn't knock me out, but I was dazed pretty bad." Kara paused and turned away. "Anyway, he had his way with me that night. Wasn't much I could do about it seeing as how I was in a stupor, and he was so strong."

"Did you get a look at the man who did this?"

"No, it was too dark," she said. "Besides, it was about that time that I passed out. Seemed like I was in and out of consciousness for the rest of the night."

"Then, what happened?"

"I reported it to the Sheriff as any law abiding citizen would, and it got swept under the rug since all evidence pointed at Harlan. Ain't nobody in town is going to stand up to a Steelman including Sheriff Miller."

Murphy glanced across the courtroom. "Now, tell me, Kara, what was John's reaction when he heard about this incident?"

"He was very concerned about me."

"Did he get mad about what happened?"

"Not that I remember."

"So, he didn't threaten the Steelman's"

"No, sir."

"Did he storm over to their place?"

"Absolutely not."

"Your witness," said Murphy returning to his seat.

Harrison slowly got to his feet. He leaned over and read notes that he had made earlier. "Now, Mrs. Watson…do you mind if I call you Kara?"

"It's Mrs. Watson to you," she said coldly.

Harrison gave a quick patronizing smile. "Now, Mrs. Watson, the way I understand it you were more than just friends with Harlan when you were kids, is that right?"

"I guess you could say that," she replied.

"Were you two going steady?"

"For a while."

"How long, a year, two years?"

"It was about two years."

"How would you characterize your relationship with Harlan during that time? Would you say you were just friends, sweethearts, lovers?"

Kara glanced at John. "I don't know. I guess we were no different than other couples at that age."

"Harrison grinned. "Well, Mrs. Watson, if you were just like other kids at that age, you most likely had sex with Harlan."

"I object, your Honor," said Murphy. "This line of questioning is irrelevant. I don't understand what Mr. Bentley is doing here."

The Judge leaned forward. "Mr. Bentley, where are we going with this line of questioning?"

"Your Honor, I'm simply trying to show the background of these two people so that we can understand the frame of mind that Mr. Watson had when he stormed over to the Steelmans' house."

"I'll allow it, but I'm warning you to be careful," said the Judge.

"Now, Mrs. Watson, would you please tell the court. Did you have sex with Harlan?"

"No, I didn't," she replied.

"Pardon me for saying so, but that seems a bit hard to believe. Here we have two young people going steady for two years and not having sex. Is this what you would have the court to believe?"

Kara smiled. "I guess you're pretty much going to have to take my word for it seeing as how I'm the only one left who knows for sure."

Harrison paused. "Good point," he said. "I'll give you that one. So, you married John, had a child, and eventually ended back here in our little town. Tell me, Mrs. Watson, did Harlan ever come by to see you?"

Kara turned to John. "Yes, he stopped by once or twice."

"Once or twice? What do you mean by once or twice? Surely, you can remember how many times an old boyfriend stopped by to see you."

"Twice."

"I'm sorry. What did you say?"

"He came by twice."

"So, Harlan stopped by to see you not just once but two times. Was John there?"

"No, sir."

"John wasn't there? Did you tell him about it?"

"Yes."

"What was his reaction?"

"He was angry."

"Angry? A former boyfriend of yours shows up twice to see you, and John is angry when he hears about it? It would seem to me that he would be down right mad. Mad enough to go find Harlan and have it out with him. Did John say anything like that?"

"John was mad, but he didn't say anything about going after Harlan," said Kara.

"So, what you're saying is that he let it slide," said Harrison walking to the middle of the courtroom. "Then, on the twenty-first when you told John about Harlan trying to rape you, that was the last straw. He stormed out of the house and probably muttered something about wanting to kill Harlan. Is that about the way it happened?"

"No, he never said anything about killing Harlan."

"Never? Not even once?"

"Never."

"Come on, now, Mrs. Watson," said Harrison. "There must have been times in your life when you've been mad enough to say something like you want to kill someone. You don't mean it, but you say it anyway. Can you remember such a time?"

"Yes, I suppose so."

"Well then, if that's the case, I'm sure you've heard John utter those same words, haven't you?"

Kara glanced at John. "Well, I guess so."

Harrison walked over to the witness stand. "So, it is true that John Watson has mentioned that he would like to kill someone. Now, let me ask you this. What was the condition of your husband when he returned home?"

"What do you mean?"

"Mrs. Watson, he just got back from having a fist fight with another man. There must have been some bruises or cuts."

"He had several bruises over his body and he was covered in blood."

"So, he obviously had been in a fight. Wouldn't you say?"

"Oh, yes," she said. "There was no doubt about that."

"Did you ask him about Harlan?"

"Yes, and he said that Harlan was alright when he left him."

"Did your husband say that Harlan was on his feet?"

"No."

"How did he describe Harlan's condition?"

"He said that Harlan was still moving."

"So, the last time John Watson saw Harlan Steelman he was lying on the floor and just barely moving as a result of a fist fight between the two men. Thank you, Mrs. Watson, you're excused."

Kara did not move. She glanced first at the Judge and then at her husband. She slowly got to her feet and returned to her seat.

John leaned over to his attorney. "I don't think we scored on that round, do you?" he asked.

"Ever play chess?" asked Murphy.

"Years ago," he replied. "Never was much good at it. Why?"

"We might have taken some heat by putting your wife on the stand. I knew that we wouldn't win that round, but I'll tell you something. We just moved our queen in position to checkmate our opponent on this move."

"I don't understand," said John with a puzzled look.

Murphy smiled. "You will, my friend," he whispered. "Your Honor, I would like to call Nolan Steelman to the stand."

The old man walked across the courtroom, was sworn in, and took a seat in the witness chair.

"Now, Mr. Steelman, I just need to ask you a few questions, and we'll have you out of that chair in no time. Okay?"

Nolan nodded his head.

"Mr. Steelman, you've known the defendant and his wife, Kara, for a long time, haven't you?"

The old man shifted his weight. "Yes, I suppose that's right. Guess I've known them since they was kids."

"In fact, Harlan and Kara dated for a while, didn't they?"

"Sure did," he said with a smile.

"How long were they together?"

The old man rubbed his face. "I guess it was about two years, maybe more."

"Did Harlan bring Kara around very much?"

"Oh, yes indeed," he said. "Harlan brought her over to the house all the time. My God, those were the sweetest days. I guess I wanted her to stay at our place all the time. I know I hated to see her go."

"Do you think Kara liked you, Mr. Steelman?"

"Yes, I think so," he replied.

"You liked Kara, didn't you, Mr. Steelman?"

"I sure did."

"In fact, wouldn't you even say that you loved her?"

The smile on Nolan's face disappeared. "What do you mean?"

"I mean didn't you love her not like a man loves his child but like a man loves a woman?"

Nolan sat up in his chair. "That's a ridiculous thing to say!" he shouted.

"Is it?" asked Murphy. He walked over to a table and picked up one of the journals. He turned to Nolan and held the book over his head. "Is it that ridiculous when you consider the things you wrote in this journal years ago?"

"Where did you get that!" shouted Nolan.

"It was obtained legally if that's what you're wondering," said Murphy dropping the book on the table in front of him. "Now, Mr. Steelman, Did you not love this woman? In spite of the vast age difference between you two, didn't you love Kara with all your heart?"

Nolan leaned back in his chair. His eyes wandered searching for the right answer. "The world seemed so innocent all those years ago," he said still staring at the floor. "She was so sweet and full of life. Her eyes seemed to laugh, and her smile was forever. Writing about my feelings in the journal seemed to help. It was a secret I could never share with anyone. No one would understand. How could a man of my age fall in love with a girl that young, and yet it seemed so right. Now, here I am sharing my most intimate and private thoughts with the rest of the world. It all sounds so dirty now."

Murphy cleared his throat. "Mr. Steelman, would you please answer the question? Did you indeed love Kara as a man loves a woman?"

Nolan blinked several times and turned to Murphy. "Yes, I loved her," he said softly. "I loved her like no other man could. I still do. Hell, I told myself not to fall in love with her. Nothing could ever come of it, but I couldn't help it."

Murphy picked up one of the journals and thumbed through the pages. "Mr. Steelman, there is an entry in your journal when you talk about another woman other than your wife. From what I read, it would seem that you were deeply infatuated with this woman, but unfortunately there are pages missing from the journal. It's as if they had been torn from the book."

Nolan seemed to relax. He took a deep breath and let it out slowly. "Those pages were torn from the book by my wife. She found the journal and ripped out the pages to confront me with them."

Murphy stepped closer to the witness stand. "Mr. Steelman, would you please tell us who the woman was?"

Nolan slowly lifted his head. He stared at Murphy and then turned to the jury. "Like a lot of kids, Harlan was a mistake," he said. "We never intended on having any more kids, but unfortunately he came along. His mother loved him. In fact, they were really close, but when she died, he changed. I knew even when he was little he was a bad seed. Always seemed like he had the devil in his eyes. Seemed like when his mother died, there was no reason for him to hold back. It seemed like he got meaner everyday, and there was nothing I could do about it. Oh, I tried all right, but all it got me was a bloody lip or a black eye. He didn't hit me at first. That came later. Really didn't matter what I said or did, it was bound to make him mad. I've always thought a lot of it had to do with his drinking, but I sometimes think he would have been just as evil without the booze."

"Mr. Steelman, could you please tell the court who the woman was with whom you had an affair?" asked Murphy.

Nolan ignored the question. He turned and looked into John's eyes. "Harlan Steelman was an evil man, he said. "God help me, but his life should have been terminated a long time ago. I sat back and watched him ruin lives in this town for too many years. I'm just as much to blame. I guess you might say it was the last straw when I saw he was going to make trouble for John and Kara. I couldn't take that. They didn't deserve that. They are such wonderful kids."

Murphy leaned on the railing in front of the witness stand. "Mr. Steelman, you killed your son, Harlan, didn't you?"

Nolan didn't move. His eyes remained on John. "I got home early from my business trip and found Harlan lying on the floor. There was blood everywhere. I could guess what had happened. I knew John had been there. I figured Harlan had done something to John or Kara, and that's why John had done this to him. It felt good seeing Harlan lying there like that, but then I soon discovered he hadn't finished the job. Harlan was still alive. I knew John was too good of a man to wantonly kill Harlan, but it wasn't a problem for me. I went to the garage and found a piece of wood and crushed his head with it. God help me, it felt good. I have no regrets about what happened that day. Hell, I can safely say that the right hand of Satan died that day. He won't bother good people like John and Kara any more."

Confusion broke out in the courtroom. The Judge slammed his gavel on his desk. "Let's have it quiet in here," he barked. He turned to Nolan. "Mr. Steelman, do you understand the severity of the statement you just made? "You have incriminated yourself in a court of law."

Nolan glanced at the Judge but said nothing.

"Mr. Steelman, if you thought so highly of John, how could you let him take the fall?" asked Murphy. He's on trial for the murder that you committed, and you let this go on without confessing. Why?"

Nolan turned away from John. "What I did is probably the most cowardly act a man can do. Letting someone else answer for your sins is despicable. I just didn't have the nerve to own up to it. I'm too old to go to prison. Hell, I wouldn't last a week in a place like that. Besides, I figured there wouldn't be enough evidence to convict John. When I saw that the trial wasn't going so good, I guess I knew deep down that the truth would eventually have to come out. After all, there was no way I was going to let him go to prison for something I did."

Nolan paused and turned to face John. "You see, I loved John as much as anyone else in the whole world because the woman I had an affair with all those years ago was his mother, Emma Watson. John Watson is my illegitimate son."

The courtroom erupted in chaos. The Judge banged his gavel as reporters ran from the room to find telephones.

Nolan's eyes remained fixed on John. "I'm so sorry, John. I hope some day you will be able to forgive me."

"Bailiff, take this man into custody," instructed the Judge. He turned and slammed the gavel on the desk. "Case dismissed!" he shouted. "The defendant is free to go."

Kara got to her feet and rushed across the courtroom. She fell into her husband's arms. "I love you," she whispered and kissed him on the lips.

"I love you too," said John. He put his arm around Kara and started for the door.

The crowd pushed its way to the rear of the courtroom. John and Kara followed along weaving through the people until they suddenly found themselves face-to-face with Nolan. The two men stopped. They said nothing until finally

John thrust out his hand. "Thanks," he said. With a smile, Nolan took his hand and shook it vigorously.

John turned to Kara. "Let's go home," he said.

◆◆◆

Shortly after the trial, John found a good-paying job in town. He and Kara bought a house and lived the rest of their lives in Bear Creek. Travis and Sara soon broke up and went their separate ways. Within a year after their separation, Sara got pregnant but never married. Travis went on to become an electrical engineer and eventually worked for NASA. Lone Wolf disappeared and was never seen again. There were many who have claimed to have seen a wolf that was the size of a man roaming through the woods, but it always seemed to disappear when they gave it a second look.

THE END

SCOTT FIELDS
THE AUTHOR

In 1966, Scott turned down a contract with the Detroit Tigers to pursue his lifelong dream of becoming a published author by earning a degree at Ohio University. In 1996 with a lifelong dream of being a writer, Scott started writing short stories. Within two years, he had four stories published. Since then, his first novel, *All Those Years Ago*, was published, *Summer Heat*, his fifth novel, was published in May 2012 and his most recent, *The Mansfield Killings*, based on a true story, was published in October 2012.

Now, Scott spends nearly all his time writing his next novel.

Scott lives in Mansfield, Ohio, where most of his novels take place, with his wife, Deb.

Visit his web site, www.scottcfields.com to learn more.

www.ingramcontent.com/pod-product-compliance
Lightning Source LLC
Chambersburg PA
CBHW050423260626
47156CB00003B/1135